MIRACLE

American Indian Literature
and Critical Studies Series

Gerald Vizenor, General Editor

MIRACLE
A NOVEL

LEO DUBRAY

UNIVERSITY OF OKLAHOMA PRESS : NORMAN

Publication of this book is made possible through the generosity of Edith Kinney Gaylord.

This is a work of fiction. Names, characters, places, and incidents are either the product of the author's imagination or are used fictitiously, and any resemblance to actual events, locales, or persons, living or dead, is entirely coincidental.

Library of Congress Cataloging-in-Publication Data

Dubray, Leo, 1947–
   Miracle : a novel / Leo Dubray.
     p. cm.
   ISBN 0–8061–3672–3 (alk. paper)
    1. Indians of North America—Fiction. 2. Self-destructive behavior—Fiction. 3. Police—Fiction.
I. Title.

   PS3604.U266M57 2005
   813'.6—dc22

                             2004058882

Miracle: A Novel is Volume 49 in the American Indian Literature and Critical Studies Series.

The paper in this book meets the guidelines for permanence and durability of the Committee on Production Guidelines for Book Longevity of the Council on Library Resources, Inc. ∞

1 2 3 4 5 6 7 8 9 10

MIRACLE

SAVE THE
LAST BULLET

Matthew stands with his back against a beige wall near a corner of the room. The sweet smell of perfume floating off the women and some of the men makes his eyes water. The odor reminds him of the sickening potpourri his ex-wife, Barbara, brought home from the Hallmark Card Shop—$2.99 a basket. Dancing particles of yellow pollen from hothouse funeral flowers and waves of chemical fumes rising from the pink—Barbara would have called it mauve—carpet infect his sinuses. Matthew looks like he's been crying.

The ritual is for Matthew's old partner, Spot— that is, Officer Richard Leroy Murphy—who, according to his obituary, ". . . died suddenly" and, according to his current wife, not unexpectedly, "after suffering a blood clot to the heart late Tuesday evening. . . . rushed to the hospital. . . . Officer

Murphy retired four years ago after a distinguished twenty-eight-year career. He was 59." His name is misspelled *Murpy* in the newspaper. Matthew saved a copy.

At the head of the room Spot is laid out, toes up, in his polished wooden box, which is equipped on both sides with decorative, gold-colored handles as if a group of his friends might carry him off to his waiting hole and lower him by hand. Of course that will not happen. Eternal Meadows Funeral Chapel and Crematory has machines to do all the lifting, carrying, and lowering that Spot and his box will ever need.

Matthew blots his eyes with the same damp wad of pink—Barbara called it fuchsia—toilet paper that he'd used earlier to blow his nose. The scented paper makes him want to sneeze, and he tosses it into a wastebasket near his corner. Barbara had bought several cases of the tissue—fifty extra fat rolls each—at Costco, where twice a month she prowls the aisles looking for specials, "my deals," she calls them. "Buying in volume saves us a fortune." On her last trip before their separation, she came home with four cases of macaroni and cheese, two blenders, discontinued models, very cheap, for backup, because "You never know," and a giant box of smoked King Salmon that Never Needs Refrigeration. She was most proud of a case—that is, five hundred bags—of Pink Peach Herb Tea. "Caffeine is a dangerous drug. Herbal is the only way to go." She sounded triumphant, as if she'd conquered something. "I love Costco. Everything is so cheap." When she finally left him, Matthew hid most of the Costco stuff from the movers to keep her from having it. Oddly, she never asked for any of the things to be returned.

Matthew needs to blow his nose. From across the room a tissue box decorated with a lavish display of lavender flowers beckons him. The box sits on a pedestal table in the middle of a group of lieutenants, captains, and deputy chiefs and their wives and husbands. He tries to take the first step toward the tissue box that will send him weaving his way through the *I'm sorry*s, the *He was a great guy*s, and the *We'll all miss him*s. Spot had known most of the brass from the old days when they were young officers together. Those in the crowd next to the tissue pedestal had moved up to offices with secretaries and free coffee, while Spot stayed on the beat. When he was alive, they hated him for not joining them and feared him for what he knew about them.

"Don't ask me anything about the old days." Spot looked at him as if his life might depend on not knowing. "If they think you can burn them, they'll come after you. You can't fight them. Don't even try."

"I need to know the truth to protect myself."

"No you don't."

"I can't react to what I don't know."

"Exactly."

Toward the end Matthew had known that Spot was going to die. He was easily distracted, as if he didn't care about the job. Just before he retired, he'd stumbled over a rise in the pavement and laughed too hard trying to be cool; even the crook was red eared. Twenty-eight years on the street, it was his last arrest.

A line of thin snot trickles out of Matthew's nose to his upper lip. He wipes it away with the back of his index finger and sticks his hand in his pants pocket.

Spot's wives arrive at the same time. The ex is escorted by her son—a tall, skinny version of Spot. The kid finds her a chair and stands next to her like a bodyguard. The current wife comes in with a guy from the funeral home—the only one with any color to his skin. The funeral guy gets her a glass of water, and she sits in a chair when he points at it. He clutches her hand and hovers with his face near hers. They speak briefly, intimately, like lovers, before he leaves her.

The two wives take awhile looking around and over and through each other, and after they stop glaring, they each take a turn to look at Spot. Matthew goes over to the ex to pay his respects. He's known her longer. She looks like a series of large wooden blocks stacked on two beefy poles. Even her jaw is square and big. Her waist is painfully cinched, like a sausage, and seems responsible for squaring off her hips and butt to match the rest of her. As he comes near her, Matthew wishes he could nod respectfully and keep going. She seems likely to explode. Before he has a chance to veer away, the ex reaches out and grabs him with both of her large, square hands. She's quick for her size. Her long fingers wrap around his forearm. "This is her doing." Her breath leaves the air with a stale, garden-mulch odor. She leans into him as if desperate to share a secret. "That bitch killed him." Smeared drops of mascara blacken her swollen eye bags. "We had a good life together, a good marriage. You know we did." She looks like a dead guy's wife, sick with loneliness and frustration. Heat from her hands burns through Matthew's coat and shirt to his arm. Spot's kid pries her grip loose. "Come visit us," she says. She says "Please" as if she'll die if he doesn't. The kid smiles like he's apologizing and escorts her out. The crowd parts for them. The stink of her soft, flowered perfume overpowers the mulch smell and forces Matthew to wipe his eyes with his finger.

The current wife sits at the front of the room near Spot's box. She wears a black dress that's tight enough and short enough to ride up on the thigh of her crossed leg. She holds a white, frilly hanky but never has the need to bring it to her eyes or nose. Her large breasts are tightly harnessed in and up high, making them look almost petite. A few days earlier at the hospital, she'd been quiet and withdrawn, not at all desperate like the ex. "He's letting himself die," she said. "He misses being part of the gang." She said it like a warning. "I can't even get him out of the house." Her voice was confident, sexy, and controlled like an actress. She's at least twenty years younger than the ex but seemed secure, more stable. After about an hour the doctor came out and told them Spot was dead.

"If you need anything." Matthew had noticed her nipples showing through her blouse. He hoped she wouldn't call.

He walks over and stands beside her at a ninety-degree angle. The same way he'd have stood with a crook on the street. "He was the best cop I ever knew."

The current wife reaches out, and her fingertips brush the back of his hand like a feather. "He said the same thing about you."

Matthew takes a step back. "Seems like I could have made it easier for him to retire."

"How?" She folds her hands around her hanky. "I don't know."

"There's nothing." She smiles. "You look handsome."

"Thanks, so do you." Before he can correct himself, she wishes him well and thanks him for coming.

"It's nice to see you. I appreciate your help at the hospital. Call me." As soon as she says it, he thinks about being naked with her in Spot's bed. Snot drips from his nose, and he hopes she doesn't notice.

He retreats to a corner of the room with a window that he discovers can't be opened. David and Edward wander over and stand next to him. David hands him a white handkerchief with an ash-colored *D* embroidered on the smooth, silky material.

Matthew blows his nose and ruins the cloth. "Sorry."

"Keep it." David turns slightly, and the fabric of his suit adjusts as if it's a living part of him. The suit is charcoal, dark enough for a funeral without bringing any tragedy to mind. The lapels are perfectly flat and masculine and seem to invite the touch of a woman's palm; his legs, arms, and waist measure exact even-numbered inches that corresponded to common sizes. All of his clothes, even his uniforms, fit perfectly without alteration. His dark, beautifully shined shoes are tasteful with an interesting line, not too formal, not too comfortable looking. Matthew saw those exact shoes but never thought to buy them for himself and probably could not have found a pair to fit. His right foot is wide and the arch is high; his left is flat and narrow. Both of David's are a perfect 11C. David's square shoulders and straight back might make another man seem aloof, military-like, but his movements are easy, casual, inviting. He nods to the current wife across the room and then turns to Matthew. "Christ, she must have used a winch to get those things flattened out." He glances back to the current wife. "Looks good enough to eat, doesn't she?"

"Give it a rest." Matthew blows his nose into David's wadded handkerchief and stuffs it into his pocket.

Edward hunkers over both of them like a hawk protecting a kill. He smiles his easy, yellow-toothed smile. The blood appears gone from his cocoa-colored face. "I'll be outside for a minute." As he walks away, his arms flap at his sides like a willow's limbs. The smell of his breath mints, his sweet cologne and cigarettes follow him like a weak shadow.

"When did he start smoking again?" Matthew's stuffy nose makes his voice sound as if he has a cold.

"Don't know."

"Hate to see it."

David shrugs. "He's old enough to know better."

Spot's kid comes back and stops Edward at the door. The kid shakes his hand like an old friend. He stays by the front door after Edward goes outside and greets people as they walk in, pointing to the refreshment table and thanking them for coming. He looks like a young Spot, but most of the people don't seem to know him.

Guys in their late thirties and forties, most just starting to gray out, some with their wives, filter in. They're like Matthew, except they're white. Most of them are older than David. They hang near the corners and watch and nod to one another. A few talk and shake hands. Like Matthew, they wear their court suits. Their wives huddle near them and smile with their lips held tight together.

Lieutenant Lopath, with his wife holding onto his arm, materializes from the crowd, dominates the room for a moment, and then glides over to Matthew and David.

"Matthew." The lieutenant stands straight while moving his free hand around the back seam of his suit jacket like a girl in a short skirt making certain that her ass is covered. He seems about to give an order. "I know that you and Spot were close. We're having a prayer meeting over at the house tomorrow night." He touches his wife's hand as if gathering courage from her. "I'll arrange time off for the two of you if you'd like to come."

His wife's eyes are blank as a cow's and shine in their own dampness as if she might drop a couple of tears. "Praise the Lord." The words pop from her mouth like an unexpected orgasm. The couple slides away and submerges back into the crowd like a pair of swamp frogs.

David smiles and pops a dime-sized breath mint. "Make a guy gag. I don't know what Ed sees in her."

"Edward is still doing Lopath's bride?"

"That's right."

"I think we should go to his goddamn prayer meeting." Matthew wipes his nose with the clean side of David's handkerchief.

"Are you nuts?"

"I'm serious."

"Shoot me if I ever go to one of those meetings."

"We'll take Edward with us."

They're still chuckling when Jake and his wife, Cindy, join them. Jake is wearing black cowboy boots that match his black suit and help to compensate for Cindy's heels. Jake and Cindy appear to be exactly the same height.

Cindy smiles. "So, Matthew, what's so funny?"

"I can't tell you."

"No balls, Matt? Balls are real important, aren't they, Jake?"

Fear shoots across Jake's face. "I guess so."

Cindy turns away from him. "I'll talk to Matthew. Tell me a story, Matthew. Tell me the right story about balls and drag racing."

Matthew looks at Jake's dead eyes.

"Don't look at him." She points at Jake with her thumb over her shoulder. She sounds disgusted.

"I don't know anything about drag racing."

"Come on, Matthew, tell me the same story Jake told me about the two of you at the races." She smiles at Matthew as if she hates him.

"Cindy, this isn't the place." Jake's voice drips with weakness as if he's losing his balls.

"Let's listen to Matthew." She sounds like she's dismissing a child.

"Cindy, shut the fuck up."

"Fuck you, Jake." She turns away from them and strolls slowly over to Spot's current wife. The two women hug and then they talk.

Matthew searches for a clean place on David's handkerchief. "I think you've been had."

Before she walks out the front door, Cindy smiles her hateful smile at Jake while waving a set of car keys with her index finger.

"You could have warned me, Jake." Matthew holds back a sneeze.

"I was going too, but I didn't think she had the balls to do that here." He shakes his head. "I'll need a ride."

The younger officers arrive in small groups—mostly threes to fives. They are everything: black, Mexican, Asian, and a few Indians. Some of them are women, some are gay or lesbian, and some are white. They all mix. The women officers are stiffer and slicker than the cops' wives, and they go where they like. A few of them even mix with the brass.

In time each of them lines up to look at Spot through his little window. His box is surrounded by stinking white and violet flowers that he would have hated, and he's dressed in his gray court suit that he also hated. Matthew passes in front of the casket in line with the others.

Spot is changed. His chin is a small button centered between jowls that sink into powdered folds of soft flesh around his neck. His hazel eyes are covered by paper-thin lids, and the bags of dark blue flesh beneath them look like faint bruises through the powder and foundation. Spot is deader than hell and looks it. There's nothing left of him.

He hadn't been fat when he was working. The extra weight came after he retired. Matthew remembers him fit and stocky, with big arms and with lots of red hair on the backs of his hands and fingers. His eyebrows had been bushy red, and the hair on his head was thick and short. He never combed it. "Can't get a comb through it," he'd say. His face was honest, pleasing, and spotted with freckles. "I'll lie when I have to do it." You could trust him. Matthew couldn't remember Spot ever lying about anything, except in court.

"It'll all be worth it when I retire." He'd said it a hundred times, maybe more.

RIDGE ROAD

Matthew opens the garage door from inside. Out front the afternoon sun beats on his four-year-old tan Honda sedan parked on the gravel driveway. Blotches of faded paint mar the hood and roof—eleven more payments. From the shadows he watches Barbara gently strap their daughter, Melanie, into the child's car seat in Barbara's silver Mercedes. The little girl holds her arms away from her sides and stares blankly like a princess being dressed by a servant. Her face is calm, almost bored; her moist lips are slightly parted, and her little brow is smooth and passive. She's a good actress. Her dark eyes are the only giveaway. They're too distant, too removed, too cool. Matthew catches bits of fear flashing in them. She could fool anybody, except her daddy.

When Barbara finishes, she shuts the car door and brushes a speck of dust from the side window with her palm. She blows a kiss to her daughter and then turns to glare at Matthew. There's a brutal darkness in her eyes that he doesn't much care for. Of course he's seen the look before, when they were together, when she had real cause to hate him. During the worst of it he slept at David's house, sometimes with a woman, and then he'd wait until he knew Barbara was gone for the day before going home. Those were the bad times, the dangerous times. He'd moved all the guns out of the house. They both agreed that they were lucky to be alive.

Her skinny, three-inch stacked heels sink into the graveled driveway, making her wobble. She could easily twist an ankle and fall. *If she goes down in the driveway, how will I touch her? By the arm? That's it, holding her up by the arm. But what if I had to carry her into the house? I'd have to touch her leg and support her back, and through her cool, cream-colored blouse one of her big tits will certainly press hard against my chest. Her face will be inches from mine. The clash of her scent, as she calls it, with the sweet spearmint gum always on her breath, will be all over me.* He remembers her wearing similar stupid shoes and bright pink toenail polish to a squad picnic the summer after they married.

She marches toward him, crunching the gravel, like she's coming right into the garage to slug him, but she stops at the shadow line next to the porch steps.

Matthew holds his spot in the dark, cool garage.

"Look at our daughter." Her voice is high like an owl's screech. "How can you do this?"

He could yell and throw the blame back at her. He's done it before. During the time when they fought every day, he'd said a lot, too much. The fighting was hateful and cheap. She burned a huge pile of his clothes on the front lawn after he pissed all over the inside of her car. He bought himself some new clothes, and Barbara's parents bought her a new car, but the hate was still there, waiting for them.

"Babs." He uses the name to demean her, but she never seems to mind. "Find a boyfriend."

Her bright blue eyes widen and flash with fury as if just now, for the first time, she is ready for the end. "What makes you think I haven't?"

How could I have ever married her or anyone like her? If she goes down, she lays where she falls.

She crunches away through the gravel. Her perfect butt juggles with each harsh step. When she reaches her car, she stops and turns back to him. "By the way, maybe this darned old house would sell if you'd clean it up. It looks like a bunch of wild Indians live here."

He doesn't yell at her to *fuck off*, because Melanie is with her.

Barbara pulls out of the driveway past the blue and red For Sale sign hanging from its own gleaming white post. She stops on the road in front of the house, and the driver's window glides down. "I want that money, Matthew. You sell this house. Don't make me go back to court."

Melanie raises her hand to wave good-bye. She looks confused, as if she wants to cry and smile all at once. *As she gets older, she'll swallow Barbara's bitterness, and someday she'll wear pink toenail polish and skinny stacked heals, and she'll hate me.*

The silver Mercedes follows a false ridge, disappearing in drifts of gray smog where the road path responds to the deep gullies scarring the mountainside, and then the car is out again as if materializing from the sticky cloud. The air is getting worse. His sinuses close, and the pressure increases to a throbbing deep in his forehead. The Mercedes vanishes around the last turn. He pops a few aspirin from a pill jar on his workbench and swallows them quickly without water.

TEPEE TIME

Ten years ago on a warm spring day Barbara Ann is late for her one o'clock biology class, but instead of hurrying along, she chooses to stroll and enjoy the sun on her back. A soft breeze brings the sweet smell of the campus-quad rose garden mixed with a bit of freshly mowed grass. She stops while crossing an open bridge walkway that connects the old red-brick science building to its new glass and steel annex. There is no reason to rush. Doctor Grey, her biology professor, has never said a single word about her coming into class late. Whether he's lecturing or giving a power-point presentation, she walks in as her mother taught her: her head high, her shoulders back, as if she owns the place. Always, the professor seems relieved. His nervous, tight face relaxes into a soft, kidlike grin as if he's been waiting for her, as if they're dating.

She comes to class late at least once a week just to see the change she causes in him.

Thick, manicured lawns mottled by maple, birch, aspen, and a few tall, straight Douglas fir surround the rose garden in the middle of the quad. The garden is a large oval with deep red blooms at the center, fading to pink and then white toward the outside. She finds Matthew sitting on the lawn near the base of the bridge. He's older, bigger, and darker than the other students and easy to pick out. He continues to stare up her dress long after she makes eye contact. At last he beckons her to join him, and she does. They sit together on the bench without touching. Their conversation drifts from classes that bore her to the unusually dry weather and then to her family and finally to his job.

"Is it hard to put people in jail?"

"Sometimes," he says, and insists that she must be very bright to miss biology classes and still pass the course.

She says she knows very little about biology but will probably get an *A*. "Aren't you afraid of getting shot or something?"

Months later when they discuss what attracted them as they stared at each other that first time— she on the bridge, he in the garden, both admit thinking the same thought: *I will have that one.* "You were staring right up my dress," she says and slaps his bare butt. "I knew you saw me, but I couldn't stop." He rolls over and nibbles around the edge of her ear. She tells him that she likes the way he does it. "You were so dark that day," Barbara giggles. "I've never seen you so dark since." Matthew shakes his head. "I never saw anything like it. You looked like a piece of ivory." Neither is embarrassed. They smile warmly at each other. Their nights together are spent at his apartment. She brings her own pillow and leaves it, and always a garment bag with a change of clothes, several pairs of shoes, and a small suitcase with her makeup, toothbrush, scented soap, body lotions, a hair dryer, curling iron, deodorant, vitamin E oil for under her eyes, a small pink vibrator, fresh bra and panties.

"It's like packing for a vacation every day."

He agrees while carry her suitcase and garment bag up the stairs to his apartment.

The next morning she uses the handrail for support while walking down the same stairs on her way to class. She gives him a weak smile from the landing. "My legs are shaking."

He stands in the doorway, wearing only his blue boxer shorts. "You're the best," he says and scratches his nuts.

"I'm leaving here weak and vulnerable."

He keeps scratching—unable to stop the itch—and watches her labor down the stairs, step by step. Within weeks they live together in his apartment.

"You're the greatest!" Barbara says it over and over again. "I really mean it."

Barbara's best friend, Patsy, is an artist and wants to know everything. Privately, Patsy calls herself a physiognomist. "Is it true what they say?"

"He's not black for Christ's sakes! He's just part Indian is all."

Patsy licks the wooden tip of one of her brushes. "Which part?"

"I thought you only painted faces."

"Bring me his photo. I'd love to do him nude."

Barbara waits up for Matthew to come home from work—four or five in the morning sometimes. She bakes deep-dish apple pie, carefully follows the defrosting instructions on the box, and waits for the sound of his car. The television keeps her from full, hard sleep—the kind of sleep from which she doesn't easily wake. When she hears him parking his car in the garage, she jumps up, quickly cuts a large piece of the pie, and warms it in the microwave. She places two scoops of vanilla ice cream on the same plate just touching the hot pie and then worries that the ice cream will begin to melt and the pie to cool before Matthew tastes it.

"Come and get it while it's still good." She sets it on the kitchen table as he comes through the front door. "It's best when it's hot and cold and fresh like this."

Matthew comes into the kitchen and seems to fill the room. He takes his jacket off and hangs it from the back of the chair. His off-duty Glock stays in its holster, belted to his waist.

Barbara watches him eat and tells him all about Patsy. "That girl Patsy is jealous." She watches the muscles in his jaw flex when he chews. "I'm so glad you're in my life." The words come slowly, with feeling, as if she's rehearsed the line, trying to get it just right.

Matthew wipes his lips with a paper napkin. "Who's Patsy?" He waits for her to answer before taking another bite. The ice cream melts into the hot pie.

IT'S A PICNIC!

On a summer Saturday during their first year together, Matthew takes Barbara to a squad picnic. They eat hotdogs and drink a few beers. Barbara wears her black leather thong sandals with skinny three-inch stacked heels. Her soft pink toenails glare against the dark sandals. She spends most of her time with Jake's wife, Cindy, Spot's ex-wife when she was his current, and Ashley, a nineteen-year-old girl—David's date. Edward is not at the picnic.

Cindy opens a beer and hands it to Ashley. "Enjoy."

The girl adjusts her cutaway tank top. "But I don't drink." She smiles. Her teeth are beautifully even and white.

Cindy looks across the picnic area at David. "You will if you stick with him, Honey."

Barbara bites off the tip of a corn chip. "Cindy, you're bad."

"Yours is no different." Cindy takes a sip of her beer. "They're all the same, including Jake. I'm just telling the truth."

Spot's wife waves an empty plastic glass at Cindy. "Stop your bitching, Cindy, and fill this for me. Easy on the ice." Beads of sweat glisten from above her upper lip.

Cindy takes the glass from her and turns it upside down to demonstrate that it's empty. "A true scotch drinker."

"That's right, Babe."

Ashley sets her full beer on the picnic table. "No, you don't understand. Dave and I are keeping it simple." She slides the beer toward Cindy. "Like, no commitments. He does his thing, I do mine."

"No commitments." Cindy raises her beer and takes a gulp. "I'll drink to that."

"I just want to be there for Dave." Ashley drags her long blonde hair to one side and sends it slithering over her shoulder.

Barbara continues to nibble at her corn chip. "I don't think I could do that without a commitment from a man."

Cindy chuckles and gives off a little cough. "Commitment is a joke. Men are scum and cops are worse."

"I won't believe you." Barbara tosses the remains of her corn chip into a trash can. "You don't know that. How could you? If it's that bad, how come you're still with Jake?"

Spot's wife takes her full glass of scotch from Cindy. "That's right, you girls don't listen to her bullshit." She blots the sweat from above her lip with a paper towel and takes two quick sips from her drink. "Spot and I have been happy together for over twenty years."

DIZZY

The next night at work, Jake calls Barbara Ann "dizzy."

"Maybe she is a little dizzy," Matthew says. "So what."

Barbara and Matthew make love every night for a year with plenty of passion and vows and promises for the future, "all eternity." Their love-making is always for a long time and loud. When they quit, they're wet and played out, and their sleep comes easily. His snoring doesn't wake her from her hard sleep. Barbara is the best piece of ass Matthew has ever had. "I love your cock," she says. She gets pregnant with Melanie, and they marry, and at least once every day one of them reminds the other, "I love you." He knows that Jake doesn't have anything like this at home.

A year after Melanie is born, the three of them, a family, move from his apartment up to the house on Ridge Road, about the time the real trouble begins. Barbara hates living away from the city. She's afraid to drive the road at night. "I feel trapped up here," she says. "What if there's a fire and you're not here? What then?"

"I don't know," he says. "Do what you'd do in the city. Call the fire department."

"What were you thinking when you moved us up here?"

Matthew doesn't bother with an answer.

MOM

Barbara and her mother spend many after-noons together, talking for hours, while lounging around the backyard patio of Barbara's childhood home—the same house she was living in when she met Matthew.

"It's so dusty up there."

Her mother sips iced tea from a tall glass and waits.

"The wind blows and blows. You don't want to go outside. None of my friends visit. It's an hour to any kind of decent shopping, and Matthew isn't much help. He comes home from work later and later."

Her mother's eyes drift to a small patch of lawn that's not as green as the rest—a place the gardener needs to work on.

"I used to feel so lucky, but now I just feel sad and guilty. I should be up there cleaning that place right now."

"Who's your toughest critic?" Her mother's voice is smooth and soothing.

Barbara smiles. "Thank you, Mother. You always make me feel better."

"That's what I'm here for."

Barbara's smile fades. "Our neighbors have chickens." She pulls her top down to cover her belly button. "Chickens for heaven's sake."

"It's a dreadful location." Her mother freshens their glasses with iced tea from a tall glass pitcher. The tea is beautifully golden and scented with dark green leaves of mint that swirl in the clear pitcher. "But then, what would you expect?"

"You're right. You're always so right." Barbara gazes across the red-brick garden patio, mottled with shade from two paper birch trees. "I love spending time with you in this place. It's so beautiful and clean."

They relax on heavy iron chairs with comfortable thick blue and white striped cushions. Their tall glasses of iced tea leave circles of condensation on coasters decorated with German and British coats of arms. Little Melanie chases white butterflies across the lawn. Finally, near the end of a long, pleasant afternoon, the offer is extended, very graciously in her mother's most elegant, refined voice. "We want to do something slightly special that I know you and Melanie will appreciate." She parts her lips and smiles. A small breath escapes from between her teeth. From anyone else it might be called a snicker, but Barbara's mother, little Melanie's grandmother, and the first-generation matriarch of a real-estate and banking empire does not snicker.

Later that night in the living room on Ridge Road, when Barbara tells Matthew, she repeats her mother's words. "She said, `something slightly special.' Could you just die?" Her parents are buying them a house, "a real home" in what her mother calls "a nice neighborhood," and "so convenient, less than a mile from us." The words hit Matthew's stomach like bad mayonnaise. The "just die" part has its own special pain.

"I've seen it," she says. She bounces over and hugs him. "The rooms are huge and clean. Perfect for decorating." She jams her breasts against his chest. "Everything about it is just so awesome." Her breath is sweet, and her lips taste like the spearmint gum she always chews. He feels her nipples harden. "I know I can make you happy there," she says.

DOUBLE-CROSS-BLOOD

From the outside Quiet Ridge Assisted Living looks like an apartment complex—two stories, passive stucco walls with lavender trim, evenly mowed and cleanly edged lawns, manicured beds of yellow and black pansies out front, with gated parking for the residents—most of whom don't drive. A tall, well-trimmed hedge secures the sides of the property. At the rear a twelve-foot chain link fence with rolled razor wire strung across the top keeps the residents feeling safe. The large automated doors at the main building part slowly as Matthew approaches. The doors are heavy with beveled glass and framed with golden stained oak. They stay open long enough for him to enter and leave several times. The place smells like Spot's funeral.

He passes a fish tank with a line of bubbles tracking up one side. A small school of neon tetras turns away from him. The receptionist nods from her stool behind a high counter. While he waits for her to finish talking on the phone, his eyes wander to the Monthly Activities calendar hanging from a bulletin board next to the counter. A color snapshot of the Resident of the Week is centered on the board: Helen Fizzlehard. Helen wears a red flowered dress that probably fit her well before her figure turned skeletal. A puff of white hair decorates the top of her head like a dollop of vanilla ice cream on a piece of pie, and her dark eyes gleam with gratitude and confusion. Matthew's father has never been Resident of the Week.

The receptionist hangs up the phone.

"Is he in his room?"

"I would say so." The phone rings. "Just a minute." Her voice takes on a slow, bouncy tone as if she's condescending to a child. "Put the tray stand in the back. If you set it out front, the residents will fall over it. We'll have trays scattered everywhere, and then we'll have to pick them all up again." She smiles at Matthew and hangs up. "Let's see." She opens a large black chart book and leafs through the pages. "I'll be . . . Martha Miller broke her walker. That woman needs to take some weight off." She chuckles. "Now, yesterday morning your father didn't eat his poached eggs, and he refused his medication. Better today, ate a scrambled egg and dry toast."

"He'll die without his meds."

"Yes, we know." Her voice drifts to the same slow, bouncy tone she used on the phone. "But if he refuses, there's nothing we can do."

"You have a notation to call me."

"I see we do, but . . ." The phone rings. "Just a minute."

Matthew leaves her talking on the phone. Her slow, bouncy voice follows him down the long corridor. The hallway carpet and the walls are creamy beige with a touch of pink mixed in like a sugary additive. Apartment doors, with permanent numbers and removable name plates, line both sides of the passage. One of the doors is decorated with a little plastic deer, another with a smiling rag doll with rosy cheeks and orange hair, and the last one before his father's displays a large brass cow-bell hanging from a hook under the name plate and a large red sign: Oxygen In Use—No Smoking.

He knocks and opens the door to his father's apartment. "Hello. Hello."

The old man sits in his recliner beside the bed. The recliner is covered with new fabric: a decorative brown and white checked weave, glossy with heavy treatments of a fabric protector.

"How are you?"

"I'm dead." Dark blood vessels spray into tiny spider webs across the pale skin hanging from his cheekbones. "This place is a death house."

"You look good."

"Compared to what?" The old man turns his large, dark eyes on Matthew. "You're a goddamn liar."

Matthew sits on the only other chair in the room. It's the last of the dining-room chairs from the old days at home. "You didn't take your meds yesterday."

"What difference does it make?"

"The nurse was concerned."

"Fuck her. Hey, you got a smoke?"

"We don't smoke anymore."

The old man grips his walker and stands up. "I'm getting out of here."

Matthew picks up a newspaper from the carpet beside his chair. "Where to?" He opens the paper and tries to read the headline.

The old man's black eyes go blank. "I wanna go home." His voice is soft and weak. He pushes the walker a few steps.

Matthew folds the newspaper and sets it back on the floor. "Why don't we stay here for awhile?"

"You stay. See how you like it." He turns his walker toward the window and stares out through the open blinds toward the evenly cut lawn and a line of weak saplings. "I ever tell you about the time I went back to the Saint Joe ranch?"

"I thought nothing but Indians lived around Saint Joe."

He backs up and slumps into his recliner. "You know I loved your mother very much."

"Yes, I know."

The old man picks up the newspaper. "I wanted her to see the place." His blank, dark eyes stare at the front page. "I always thought it would be me to go first."

Matthew shifts his weight, and the chair's loose joints squeak.

"Would have been easier." The old man opens the paper as if he's reading it. "Christ, there was nothing left at Saint Joe."

"When did you make the trip?"

"Right after we were married. I had to be honest with her."

"About what?"

"You ever wonder why you look more Indian than your mother?" He keeps his face buried behind the paper.

"Crossed my mind."

"You don't have to wonder about it anymore."

Matthew looks beyond the old man to the framed family pictures scattered on the wall behind him. "Why bother telling me all this now?"

"Listen to me. I worked every day in their stinking, goddamn packing factories." The old man rolls the paper into a pipe shape and holds it above his head like a club. "You think I'd have made manager if the bastards had known what I am?" He brings the paper down to the side of the chair. "Where would I be without my pension?" He rocks himself back and forth. "I couldn't afford this place. You ever think about that?"

In one of the pictures that hang from the wall, Matthew finds himself as a little boy. His mother stands behind him, holding him by the shoulders. *Your father is a good provider.* She said it often. *Don't forget it.*

"Be damned or not, I feel relieved that you know." He nods his head and continues his rocking. "Work hard, Matthew. You'll need every dime." The newspaper falls from the old man's hand to the carpet. "It's hell to be old. Don't ever get old."

CAVE DWELLERS

A mustard-colored haze hangs over the city. Another sticky afternoon ends with a blazing red sunset, too hot for the middle of March and no sign of a break. A few long, narrow clouds streak the west like hateful jagged slashes. Several years earlier the chamber of commerce spent a lot of money featuring the sunsets in an advertising campaign to stimulate tourism and new industry. The slogan: Too Beautiful To Be True, with a glossy color photo of a violet, day-ending sunset burst, appeared on the cover of the city's magazine, *New Western Horizons.* Within days reports surfaced identifying air pollution as cause for the beautiful color. The campaign continued with a new cover story using women in business as examples of diversity and no mention of sunsets. The new slogan—The Land of Many Uses—appeared under the photo of a stylish businesswoman carrying a dark brown leather briefcase and looking at a vacant acre of freshly bulldozed land.

Matthew turns his police car from the quiet street and drives to the entrance of an abandoned grade school—red brick, two stories with a red tile roof, built a generation ago as a high school. He guides the car around a crumpled twelve-foot chain link gate that's overgrown with withered crawling vines and hidden by the gnarled limbs of a giant black oak.

The asphalt glitters with fine particles of clear window glass and green specks from shattered wine bottles. He drives slowly around a pile of large gears with rusting teeth and lets the small branches from a dry bush scrape across the 911 Protect and Serve motto stenciled on the right front door. He finds his way around the char of a burned-out campfire circled by chunks of cement and old car tires used for seats. Matthew takes his place with a cluster of three other police cars parked in the shadow of an ancient willow whose fallen leaves make a soft, damp bed covering the root-buckled asphalt. From outside the willow's shadow the police cars and officers are nearly invisible. They call the place the cave, and they believe they are the only four cops on the force who know about it.

"She thinks the money is endless." Jake paces in front of the other cops. His legs are too short for his body, but his bouncing steps make him seem tall. Dark, curly hair from his square-built chest swirls up around his neck as if trying to compensate for his thinning scalp hair. With each bounce he slams his fist into his palm. More dark hairs tangle on the backs of his thick hands and fingers. Jake is a good man in a fight.

Matthew nods to Edward. "What's the matter with him?"

"He gave Cindy some cash for their vacation at Disneyland next week and she spent it." Edward lights a cigarette and inhales deeply. "Now she wants more." Smoke drifts from his mouth with each word like breath on a winter day.

"Why doesn't he tell her to forget about the trip?"

"The kids."

Jake kicks at a small pile of ruptured asphalt.

"She's never been trustworthy." Matthew sips his coffee.

"No, never."

"I wonder why he keeps trusting her."

"Who knows." Smoke from Edward's cigarette disappears, but the smell stays in the air.

Jake picks up a chunk of the loose asphalt and throws it at the willow. He walks over to the tree, peels a piece of broken bark away, and pisses on the bare tree flesh. Before they were married, Jake talked a great deal about Cindy. "She's perfect," he said. "Doesn't know another cop or anybody at the department."

Edward touches Matthew's arm and nods toward a guy in dark blue coveralls standing by the corner of the school building. The guy waves to them. Matthew unsnaps his holster strap and stays behind the police car. Edward beckons the guy to come over to them. The cigarette falls from his fingers, and he crushes it under his shoe.

The guy scratches at his gray chin stubble as he walks over to them. "God, look at this mess." His round belly stretches the coveralls tight, and the side buttonholes are frayed and blown open. He looks like an overfull balloon that might explode at any moment from the pressure. "You boys are probably wondering what I'm doing back here." He looks eye to eye at Edward and smiles at him as if they're old friends.

Edward lights another cigarette and offers him one.

The guy shakes his head. "Gave 'em up years ago. Put on a few pounds as you can see, but I'm still alive." He takes a red bandanna from his front pocket and blows his nose. He sniffles like a small boy and blows again. "They're going to tear my building down." The guy turns and faces the school. "We built it with the best bricks, double-sided interior walls, tight-grain oak floors. You can't even buy wood like that anymore. Not even in Japan." He points at the willow and waves his red bandanna like a flag before stuffing it back into his pocket. "We even changed the plans a bit to save that tree. Makes nice shade, doesn't it? We knew it would." The guy looks at them as if he knows they can't care. "A man's life don't mean nothing." He walks back the way he came without turning to say good-bye.

The police radio makes a soft click that lets Matthew know a call is coming. The call is for an officer named Bidwell. The computers are down, and the dispatcher asks him to call in for a phone number.

"I'm thinking Bidwell's new chippy is trying to call him." Jake finishes his coffee and flips the Styrofoam cup into the brush. "He says she's beautiful. `Hair like fine, silky gold.' I think he's in love. What an asshole."

David looks up from his relaxed slouch behind the wheel of his police car and raises his cell phone.

Edward slaps his hand hard on his rooftop. "Do it, David."

David smiles and makes the call to the radio dispatcher—her name is Molly, but she's known as *David's Dispatcher.* Matthew met her off duty once at a vice cop's retirement party. The vice cop was leaving the department early to manage a hunting lodge in Idaho. "It'll save the marriage," the vice cop said and downed a shot of Jack Daniels. "Great schools. Clean air." His eyes dampened from the shot. "No niggers." Matthew slid away from him and touched Molly on the shoulder. He asked if she wanted a drink.

He remembers her skinny legs and her long, sexy nose. He thinks about her nose every time she assigns him a call. At the party after he'd asked if she wanted the drink, her nostrils flared like she was searching the wind for something— trying to smell it. The nostrils were pink and clean inside. She sniffed and mentioned her husband. "He plays games," she said. "Dungeons and Dragons like some kid." When she spoke, she inhaled deeply again and again. Finally her eyes widened as if she sensed something, and then she laughed at him. He thought she might be crazy, and he was about to slide away from her like he'd done with the vice cop. "A vodka collins, if you don't mind." She inhaled deeply at him, and he made his way to the bar thinking about screwing the crazy dispatcher with her pink nostrils flared wide. He wondered if she'd give him preferential treatment with call assignments, but when he returned with the vodka collins, he saw her leaving the party with David. She turned and flared her nostrils at him one last time, and she laughed loud enough for him to hear from across the room.

David slouches down in his car seat. He softens his voice to a smooth bass and caresses the phone, urging the number from Molly, digit by digit. "Wednesday is good," he says. He writes a digit on his pad. "After work." Another digit. "What are you wearing?" He smiles as he writes a digit. "Of course I remember. Do you?" Two digits. "I said after work." He stares out the window past the other men as if he's lost interest. "How could I forget?" He writes the last number on his pad. "That's right. After work." He presses the off button on his cell phone. "I got it," he says and waves the scrap of paper. "That woman is out of her mind."

Jake rubs his jaw. "Bidwell's been working on this new chippy for months. She won't go for it."

David dials the number.

Edward grinds his cigarette butt out on the crumpled asphalt. "Five, he gets her."

Jake squints at him and nods his head slowly as if he knows something the rest of them don't.

"Is that a *yes*?"

"Make it ten."

David shifts away from the open window and speaks softer and lower than he did with Molly. "Why not?"

Jake smiles at Edward.

The radio clicks again, and Matthew knows the call is his and he's right. He's always right about calls. It's Molly. She gives him the address. Her voice is smooth and solid with a late-night texture common for people who sleep during the day.

Matthew finishes writing the address. "Damn burglary report." The victim's house is located in the only neighborhood on his beat without cars parked on lawns, with houses that don't need paint, or with trees on the parkways too big to butcher.

David nestles the phone close to his lips. "You can do anything you want," he says. "Have anything you want."

Molly gives Matthew more information. "The victim was found by her daughter. Ambulance responding." Her voice is even and seductive.

"She must think David is listening."

"Sounds more like a robbery," Edward says. "I'll roll with you."

David smiles. His cell phone seems like it's part of him, as if he was born with it attached to his ear. "Time starts now, Baby."

Edward holds his hand out, and Jake slaps it with a ten-dollar bill. "I should know better than to bet against that guy."

David tosses his cell phone onto the seat. "She's real quality. I don't know what she's doing with a bag of shit like Bidwell."

Matthew lets his car roll over to David's. Their rearview mirrors nearly touch. "I'll believe it when I see it."

"Fair enough."

Matthew and Edward follow David through the lot and down the driveway, leaving Jake alone, pacing in front of the willow and kicking at chunks of loose asphalt.

JUST THE FACTS

Photos of small children, each in their own frame—one wearing a cowboy hat posed on a pony, another in a pink dress in front of a cake with four candles—stand on an end table near the couch. Teenagers in prom dresses and tuxedos, a young soldier with a stupid tough-guy look, and couples and families decorate the top of the piano and the hallway walls. All of them are dark-haired Chinese, except for one blonde woman about thirty with her arm around an old bald guy who wears thick-lens glasses and displays a large, bright smile.

The old lady sits on an overstuffed chair in her living room with her daughter kneeling beside her. Her lips are broken open and black with dry blood. One eye is swollen closed. Her hands are dark blue and swollen. They don't look like hands at all; they look like industrial rubber gloves. She speaks Chinese to her daughter.

"They put a sewing basket over her head," the daughter says. She looks at her mother and moans, rocking back and forth on her knees. "That's how we found her. With her hands tied behind her back. I thought her head was gone. They bound her feet."

The old lady's eyes are familiar and calm. Her bloated hands rest on the arms of the chair. They look as if she may lose some of the fingernails.

"Can she identify any of them?"

The daughter stops rocking. Her face is the color of soft, gray ash. "They put the basket over her head as soon as she opened the door." Her eyes are lifeless, like a killer's. "How could she see them?"

The old lady speaks a few words to her daughter.

"One has a cross tattooed between his eyebrows. And one of the girls who kicked her was wearing gold slippers. That's all."

Two ambulance attendants lift the old lady onto a gurney. One puts a pillow on her chest and gently places her hands on it. They wheel her out. A tech-crew investigator dusting for fingerprints around the front door moves back out of the way.

"She's eighty-two," her daughter says. "You should find them and kill them."

Edward comes out from the backyard. "They left themselves a way out. The back door was unlocked, but they never bothered to use it. What's missing?"

"I got a list, clothes and jewelry. The place smells like mothballs. The stink will stay with the clothes for awhile." Matthew checks a few boxes on the report form: Motive, *Personal Gain*; Weapon Used, *Tape and a Sewing Basket.* "She's been tied since last night. Shit her pants. Could have died. They brought their girlfriends along, sort of like a shopping trip."

"Goddamn."

"Call Jake. He can help us talk to the neighbors."

"He's already doing it."

BEYOND
REASONABLE DOUBT

Matthew makes his way into the cave toward the willow tree. As he turns to avoid a pile of old truck tires, his headlights flash over David's patrol car. He parks beside the passenger door and reviews his notes from the robbery. "It was a bad one." He finishes the description of a possible suspect vehicle supplied by one of the neighbors and glances over at David's car. A young woman wearing a patrolman's hat smiles back at him. Blonde hair hangs to her shoulders from under the hat. She slides out from behind the wheel and walks around to Matthew's car. Except for the hat and black combat boots, she's nude.

"Hi Matthew," she says. She leans down and nestles her bare breasts on Matthew's arm. "I'm Mindy."

"Like your outfit."

Mindy smiles. "If I had my nipples pierced, I'd have worn the badge." She snaps her gum and blows a large pink bubble. After a moment she pops it with the long, dark-polished nail of her index finger and gathers the gum back into her mouth with the same finger. "I'm Bidwell's chippy."

"Figures." Her smell is heavy and sweet like her breasts, and he knows he'll smell her for a long time after she's gone. "Not the first time you've done that trick with your gum, is it, Mindy?"

"I'm good with my mouth," she says. "You want a blow job?"

He remembers Barbara. Her face was bright like Mindy's during their early days together. She'd call him "my he-man," and then she'd go down on him. Barbara had a great sense of humor.

David slides up from the passenger's seat and looks over at him. "Don't ever doubt me."

NIGHT VISION

The old Chinese lady turns the channel to her late-night movie. She's happy to see it's a Western, easier to follow than some of the newer movies that make no sense. A white man with a spotted horse is having some trouble. He gets drunk and another man—a Mexican—steals the horse for a gift to his girlfriend. Even though the actors speak too fast for her to understand, she keeps the sound turned on to give the pictures reality. The white man stains his skin dark brown and pursues the thief into Mexico. He finds his horse, and just before he gets away, the Mexican captures him. These two men—the Mexican thief and the white man with stained skin—have a long conversation in a bar. The thief is drinking from a small glass, and he eats a bit of lime after each swallow. They arm wrestle, and the Mexican wins. He keeps the white man hostage, but after awhile the Mexican's girlfriend helps the white man escape. The girlfriend is very beautiful, but she is not faithful to the Mexican, and she willingly accompanies the white man. As they run, the white man's brown color fades from his face. The Mexican pursues them, but it's obvious that the white man and his new girlfriend will win the battle that is sure to come.

The old woman looks away from the television to the framed pictures on the table beside her chair. She reaches out and lets her fingertips touch the last picture taken of her husband with their daughter. Her eyes wander to a yellowed black and white of her with her husband that was taken the day they left China. The doorbell rings. She smiles. Who but her daughter would come to visit so late?

PROOF

"The neighbors didn't see nothing." Jake moves his ever-sharp across the report, checking boxes, writing the neighbor's names and addresses and phone numbers. "Except maybe the guy next door. I'm leaving a notation for the detectives."

"You think he saw something?" Matthew finishes off his coffee.

"Probably, but he's scared." Jake uses the erasure. "Do you spell residence with an *S* or a *C*?"

"Try the *C*." Matthew jams the empty Styrofoam cup under the front seat.

"I need to make a list of these words."

"Couldn't hurt."

Edward turns into the cave, parks, and walks over to Matthew and Jake. "Coffee." He sets a carry-out tray with four Styrofoam cups on Matthew's hood. "Where's David?" He tears a lid from one of the cups and stirs in some powdered creamer.

Jake floats the lid to his coffee into the brush like a Frisbee. "Not here. Maybe he's hiding."

"Been and gone," Matthew says.

"How did she look?"

"As good as it gets."

Jake blows on his coffee and sips at it. "Could be bullshit, Ed. I never seen her."

Matthew sniffs at his sleeve and waves it under Edward's nose.

Jake catches a whiff. "That could be a set-up," he says.

Edward smiles. "Smells like proof to me."

THE TWO WEENIES

Bonnie strolls through the side door of Willie's Hotdogs. The screen door slams behind her. She lights a cigarette and leans back against the Honk for Service sign nailed to the building. A cloud of her smoke mixes with thick gray steam boiling from the kitchen window. She looks over at Jake and Matthew sitting in the police car and lets her eyelids go lazy. The cigarette slips from her fingers, and without looking away from the two cops, she crushes it under the sole of her dirty white sneaker. Her wide hips make a full, round curve below her thick waist, and when she finishes smoothing the rounded humps slowly with her palms, she throws her shoulders back and checks to see if the pencil is still jammed in her frizzy blonde hair. Bonnie has been told that she looks like Jane Mansfield.

Matthew groans. "I wish she'd come up with a new act."

Masses of white ruffles on the front of her blouse jiggle as she glides over to the police car. The front of her tight white pants—stained the same sickly gray as the steam rolling from Willie's kitchen window—supports a doughy fat roll under her belly button.

"Matt, try to be a little cordial."

"You have no integrity."

"You're wrong." Jake winks at Bonnie. "It's pride that I lack."

"It's both."

"You know any other cop getting free hotdogs at Willie's?"

Bonnie comes up to Jake's window and leans down toward the door. Her ruffles rest against his arm. She brings the sweaty smell of boiled hot dogs smeared with mustard and relish. "How you boys doing this evening?" She keeps her voice low and sweet, like an aging movie star. A three-inch scar of folded red flesh from an old knife wound glows on her forearm like a warning.

"Not as good as you, Bonnie." Jake gives her a genuine smile with a hint of something more than just friendship.

"He's always got something to say back, don't he, Matt?" The tip of her pink tongue brushes the rough edges of her yellowed front teeth.

"He's a real hoot, Bonnie."

"I just love him." She squeezes Jake's forearm and holds the squeeze as if her meaning goes far beyond casual, friendly love. She has told her best friend, "Me and Jake have something beyond words."

A faded green Ford with bald tires and bad shocks rolls into the lot. The driver is careful to miss most of the deepest potholes. A rusted-out fender rattles with each bump, and the muffler scrapes on the high spots. The guy parks near a broken board fence that separates Willie's from Clarence Freewater's Holiday Auto Sales in the next lot. He looks up at the Honk for Service sign, slowly gazes around the lot, everywhere except at the police car, and taps his horn.

Bonnie groans and lifts her head over the top on the police car. She yells using all of her thick gut. "Keep your shirt on, Buster! Can't you see I'm busy?" Her ruffles shake violently.

"I know a blues singer who'd give his leg for a voice textured like that." Matthew looks over at the tag on the Ford's license plate. It's expired.

Jake shakes his head. "I know what you're thinking."

"I pay for my license tags. Don't you?"

"Leave it alone."

"Why should we treat him any different than anybody else?"

"What's eating you, Matt? You don't like your free hot dogs?"

Bonnie looks back at Jake and smiles. "What are you guys talking about?"

"The difference between pride and integrity."

"Leave it, Matt."

"I better take your order, Honey, before that bozo drops a litter." She removes her pencil from her hair and holds it to write on the pad like an old-time secretary. The sleeves on her blouse hang low and open, exposing the wide sides of her red bra, the same red as her lipstick. "What'll it be?"

"That depends on who's steaming the dogs." Jake brushes Bonnie's ruffles with his elbow.

"You know I wouldn't let anybody else touch your dogs."

"We'll have two double dogs and a couple of cokes." Jake smiles like a delighted child.

Bonnie writes the order and wets her red lips with the tip of her tongue. "You mean you both want two weenies in one bun?"

THE SMELL OF CIVILIZATION

The three taillights on the left side are dark, and the three on the right sputter weakly like an engine trying to start. Red lights from the police car glare off the dark heads inside—two girls. Bidwell calls in the stop. He points the spotlight at the inside rearview mirror and jams his citation book into his back pocket. The girl on the driver's side adjusts the mirror to avoid the light from the police car and then places her hands carefully back on the wheel. Bidwell shines his flashlight on the backseat and floor and then the front seat and the passenger's hands and face and then into the driver's eyes. He expects the smell of burning marijuana or a spilled beer and hopes for neither. The reports and booking would take the rest of the night; he'd miss his lunch. The driver looks away from the light and rolls the window down.

The smell of mothballs leaking from inside the car can't be ignored.

A half hour later Bidwell and Matthew meet in a deserted shopping-center parking lot. Broken glass from the shattered lights glitters on the asphalt. One of the light poles is down. The store windows are covered with large sheets of plywood. Graffiti decorate the walls of the buildings and give the center its only color.

Bidwell leans against the hood of Matthew's car. "I can do this two ways." He rolls to one side and farts. "I can book these two little sluts, or I can give them to you."

"I'd like to talk to them."

"I know you would, but if I book 'em, that won't be possible, now will it?"

"What is it you want, Bidwell?"

"You know what I want."

Matthew considers making him say it. "She might not want to see you after knowing David."

"That's your problem."

Twenty minutes later David's car rolls into the lot and stops beside Matthew. "How'd he know it was me?"

"Who else would do it?"

David smiles. "Who else could?"

Mindy leans over and kisses David on the cheek. "I had a real blast, Baby." She bounces out of the car, and her light cotton dress dances high on her thighs. On her way to Bidwell's car she skips past Matthew like a little girl. "He's so cute."

GOOD COP

Matthew sits in the dark watching through the one-way mirror while David questions the girl wearing gold-colored slippers.

David holds a clear plastic evidence bag with a lady's yellow scarf inside. "Looks like nice material." He brings the bag close to his nose.

The girl slouches in her chair. "You want it?" She puts her feet up on the table. "It's yours. Anybody could have a scarf like that."

David sniffs the bag like a hound on the trail. "Kind of funky. I can smell it right through the plastic."

"If you don't like the smell, you should leave it alone."

"It's strong. What makes a smell like that, Yolonda?"

"How should I know?" Yolonda raises her arms and stretches. She fakes a yawn.

"The color matches your slippers."

"So? That don't mean nothing."

"It's your scarf, right? You were wearing it."

"That fat cop with the bad breath, he told you that? He's a liar."

YOLANDA
AT THE RIVER

"She's just five years old." Yolonda's mother glances down as she talks. "I don't know where she could be." The mother is eighteen. She looks like a high-school cheerleader except for her dull, guilty eyes. She smiles as if she's unsure how to react. "It happened once before." She sits on the edge of a yellow and brown plaid couch with wooden armrests and pushes stuffing back into a fist-sized tear in the thin, dusty fabric. The clear varnished finish on the wood part of the armrest is sun blistered yellow and pealing. "She's wearing her little pink dress. We were just going out."

The mother's boyfriend slouches beside her. His red, armless T-shirt exposes the fresh welts of a black laughing skull tattoo on his right bicep. The tattoo's caption—Born to Lose—is scrolled in red that matches his T-shirt. "We been all over the neighborhood, man."

"Some tattoo," Matthew says.

The boyfriend tears the filter from a cigarette. "You like it?"

"Bet it cost."

"Can't take your scratch with you, man." He lights the cigarette with a large stainless-steel Zippo and inhales deeply. "Might as well spend it on what I want." He blows his smoke over the coffee table. "Look man, the little shit pulls this crap whenever we're set to go out." Smoke continues to drift from his nose. "She could be anywhere."

Matthew calls for more officers and sends the mother and her boyfriend back to search the neighborhood. He walks the half block to a creek— usually dry—now swollen with fast brown water from the spring runoff. It stinks like an oil barrel. He avoids the soft, muddy undercut along the bank. The ragged edge looks as if large chunks of earth have fallen and disappeared into the water. A grand fir—a fifty footer—leans over, waiting to fall. He walks the upper edge of a brush wall thick with thistles, buttonbushes, and prickly poppies.

Yolanda sits on a rock near the brown, swirling water. She throws a handful of leaves and watches them spread and rush away downstream. The rock where she sits is being undercut and may fall this year or next or now. Matthew crashes through the brush down toward the water. He keeps his hands in front of his face; the brush tears at him, wedges between his gun and holster. He feels the piece leave him, and he reaches for it. Brush slaps his face hard; a sharp edge gouges his cheek. The gun slips away; he keeps fighting the brush, slashing his way down toward the edge where the little girl sits with her feet dangling. He breaks free, twenty feet from her. The little girl looks back at him and disappears. He slides to the water's edge, chest down in the mud, and reaches into the cold, brown water. Nothing, and then hair, like long, soft grass, tangles through his fingers like magic. He pulls her free.

WALKING ON WATER

Matthew walks into the interrogation room and shuts the door. The room is too small for the three of them. David slides his chair back and leaves.

"I'll keep this simple." Matthew pushes a paper tablet and a pen in front of Yolonda. "You and your friends ripped off an old lady last night. I need their names."

"You're crazy."

"If you don't give them up, the girl you were with tonight will, and we only need one of you."

"I got nothing to give up."

"Yes you do. If that old lady dies, you may never get out."

"So?" Yolonda picks up the pencil. She draws the outline of a person's head. "There's worse things."

"Not many."

"The old bitch might not die."

"It's still serious. They may even hold you as an adult."

"No way." She keeps drawing without looking up. "You're trying to scare me."

"You need to consider all the possibilities."

"I don't think so."

"You know who I am?"

"You expect me to thank you?" Yolonda looks at the pad as she draws.

"No."

"It was your job, right?"

"That's right, my job."

Yolonda sets her pencil down on the table and smiles. She slides the drawing toward Matthew.

A frightened face, a younger likeness of his own, stares back at him from the pad.

"Recognize that guy?" Yolonda laughs. "I never seen nobody so scared." She leans across the table. Her face comes close to his. "I'll tell you what you want, Cop, but this clears my debt. We're even."

IA

The red and white sign from Red's Donuts lights the six empty parking spots in front of the shop. The smell of fresh donuts boiled in oil soaks the neighborhood. In the shadows off to the side of the building, Matthew and Ed sit in Matthew's police car sipping thin coffee from Red's Styrofoam cups. A white bakery bag full of maple bars sits between them.

Ed reaches for the bag and opens it.

"Don't touch." Matthew stirs his coffee with a red plastic straw.

"What do you care? They're on Red."

"We'll need every goddamn one of them."

Headlights flash across their faces before going out. Ed blocks his eyes with his hand. "Damn fool."

Sergeant Whit's rearview mirror clears Matthew's by an inch. "Evening, boys." Whit turns away from them and squints into the shadows. White fleshy folds lap one another and hang over his collar where his neck should be. He cocks his large head—a head too big for his body—as if trying to see around the back corner of Red's. He turns back toward them. "How long you boys been here?" His yellowed eyes bulge at them.

"Long enough to get coffee."

Whit's glance wanders through the interior of Matthew's car and stops on the white bakery bag. "You can't be too careful." He lowers his voice to a whisper. "Internal Affairs."

Matthew hands him a Red's Styrofoam coffee cup. "It's a Red's Great Big." Matthew uses two hands to pass it.

"Not too much cream, right?"

"It's just the way you like it, Sarge," Edward says.

"Well now, thank you, boys." Whit's bulging eyes stay on the white bakery bag. "You guys got something going on?"

"One of the scum that did that old lady rolled over. We got a house."

Whit sips his coffee. "What did the detectives say?"

Edward hands the white bag to Matthew. "You want a maple bar, Sarge?"

"That would sure hit the spot." Whit shoves his beefy hand into the bag. "They're stuck together," he says. "I got two."

"That's all right." Matthew stirs his coffee with a red plastic stick. "We've got lots of them."

Whit expertly jiggles the two maple bars apart and takes a huge bite from the one with the most icing. He points to his mouth and garbles, "Good." A moment later he swallows hard and takes another sip of coffee. "Maple bars make a man greedy." He nibbles at the ragged edge of his bite mark like a mouse.

"We need your clearance to leave the district to work with the detectives." Matthew tosses his red plastic stir-stick under the seat.

Bits of brown maple frosting stick to Whit's thick blue lips like small festering sores. "Who's got the case?" He shoves the last of the maple bar into his mouth.

"Stan Holloway." Matthew hands the bag to Whit. "You want another?"

Whit finishes chewing and swallows. "Wouldn't say no." He takes the bag. "You call Holloway. We'll leave it up to him."

"Keep the bag, Sarge." Edward slides down in his seat and stares out the passenger window.

Whit crumples the top of the bag closed. "Thanks, I'll save the rest for my lunch." He licks his lips and some of the brown frosting falls onto his uniform shirt. "One more thing." He lowers his voice, and the red-veined webs in his yellowed bulging eyes expand. "Don't repeat what I told you about watching out for Internal Affairs." He squints at them as if he's trying to focus.

Edward sits up and looks over at him. "We won't, Sarge."

"Not a word." Matthew winks and starts his engine. He lets the police car roll to the street and stops before pulling into traffic. "What a fucking weenie."

"Amen, brother."

THE OUTLAW

The mothball smell leaks from around the front door. A skinny young guy with a shaved head, wearing an armless black T-shirt that hugs his bony chest and slim waist, answers Matthew's knock. His innocent blue eyes move from Matthew to Edward and back to Matthew. "What do you want?" he says. "We didn't call the heat."

"I know." Matthew leans into the door and hits the guy hard in the guts with the end of his flashlight. The kid groans and goes down. Matthew rolls him over, puts a knee into his back, and cuffs him. Edward steps around them and moves into the house.

Stan Holloway stands in the doorway looking down at Matthew and the handcuffed kid. "How's the interview going, Matt?"

The back door crashes in—glass breaks, wood molding splinters. Matthew stands and lifts the guy to his knees. "Maybe you'd like to take over while I go help out."

"My pleasure." Holloway turns his attention to the kid. "Love your do, friend." He rubs his own bald head. "Mine is a natural."

The kid's face is flushed. "Fuck you," he says. His voice is full of angry fear.

Holloway helps him up off the matted carpet and directs him into the living room to a red three-cushion couch with bricks for legs. Some of the stains on the cushions are slick and black, while others are crusty brown. Together, the three cushions form a rough smile.

"What's your name?"

"I got nothing to say to you."

"Now that's regrettable."

The kid looks away.

"Come on," Holloway says. "The cops will make fun of you if you don't give me your name. Pick one you like, anything."

The kid squirms into his cushion. "Can you take these off?" He moves his hands around, exposing the cuffs.

"No, but I can make them quit hurting." Holloway bends forward and loosens the cuffs. He double locks them and then sits back on the only other piece of furniture in the room—a bent-rod kitchen chair with a torn plastic seat. He bounces, using the natural spring formed by the design of the chair. "We used to have a whole set of these when I was a kid." He keeps bouncing. "Hell, this could be one of them."

"It ain't that old."

Holloway stops bouncing. "You're a funny guy."

"Not as funny as you."

"And you're quick for a kid without a name."

"Fuck you."

Matthew and Edward herd three guys in cuffs down the hallway.

"Here they come. Last chance."

"Up yours, old man."

"Boys, I must be losing my silver tongue." Holloway stands and lifts the kid to his feet. "He won't even tell me his name."

"A real live outlaw." Edward lights a cigarette.

Matthew waves a clear evidence bag with a necklace and a man's ring. "It don't matter. We got these and a pile of the victim's clothes. Most of it in the outlaw's room."

Edward exhales a cloud of smoke. "No breaks for the outlaw."

"An outlaw ain't got no friends."

Holloway shakes his head. "I told you to give up a name." He grabs the kid by the arm and directs him to move over with the others. "You got a lot to learn about being a crook."

The kid squirms and pulls free of Holloway grip. "What's the big deal, you old shit bag?"

"You're looking at some big state time, boy. More than just a couple of years."

The kid laughs and then stops suddenly as if his laugh is an act. "You don't you get it, do you?"

Holloway watches a fire light in the kid's eyes. "It's in my blood."

"You want to go to prison?"

"Don't matter what I want." He turns his back to Holloway. "I was born for it." The kid falls into line with the others. "By the way, my name is Billy. Maybe you heard of me." He looks over at Matthew. "The next time you and that fucking redskin bang on my door, I'll have something for both of you."

Holloway shakes his head. "A lot to learn, kid."

THE HEALING PLACE

The air is flat and artificial, like plastic.

"How is she?"

"Not good. Not bad." The nurse is tall, long legged with a fine jawline, maybe thirty. She could have been a model. Her nameplate is partially hidden—Nancy War . . . She fondles a blue ballpoint pen, rolling it with her thumb and index finger the way he might touch a woman's nipple. "Do you want to see her?"

He watches her play with the pen and thinks she'll probably look at his crotch, but she keeps her eyes on his. "Yes, I would."

She leads him down the quietly lit hall. The soft squeak of her shoes echoing off the walls is the only sound. Nancy opens the door to the old lady's room. "Stop by the desk on your way out."

As she walks away her hips sway to the squeak of her shoes.

The faint odor of mothballs drifts from the dark, cool room. The daughter sleeps curled in a chair with a brown hospital blanket tangled around her.

The old lady's dark eyes open as if she's been expecting him. "Please sit."

A small suitcase and woman's purse take up the space on the only other chair. "I can't stay long. I didn't know you spoke English."

"I'm sorry I have nothing to offer you."

"I don't need anything."

"You've been successful."

He nods, and the old lady closes her eyes.

"You should know," she says. "The girl with the golden slippers only pretended to kick me. The rest of them were not so kind." Her voice drifts away.

"Thank you," he says. He shuts the door quietly and makes his way down the hallway to Nurse Nancy's station.

She puts her pen down and watches him come closer. "Who is she?"

"A victim."

Nurse Nancy smiles. "Aren't we all." Her teeth are even, beautifully white, exactly like Barbara's.

"I suppose."

"Why would anybody hurt an old lady?"

"I should have asked them. Would you go out with me?"

"I knew you were going to ask." She looks down at the desk top and smiles. "I'd really like that, but I have a boyfriend." When she mentions her boyfriend, she whimpers as if suffering a stabbing pain. "I'm trying to be good."

"I understand."

"It's hard. Isn't it?"

"Yes, it's very hard."

"It's hard." She repeats the words as if she's resigned to endure and suffer.

"Impossible."

"I really am trying."

When he was younger, Matthew would have suggested some bullshit about meeting as many new people as possible to enrich her final, important choice. He'd have told her that she was special and that her boyfriend was lucky. He'd have asked her why she became a nurse, and he would have seemed interested when she answered. *Have you ever done any modeling?* Finally, he'd have suggested that she take a short break and find a quiet place so they might continue talking as friends.

"Good luck." Matthew turns to go.

"Bye." She lets out a slight moan. "Say, do you know a cop by the name of David? I never knew his last name. He's got light hair, almost blond. And he's a real sharp dresser."

Matthew turns back to Nurse Nancy's counter. "Your boyfriend is a lucky guy." He leans in against the counter, making himself comfortable. "You know that, don't you?"

She uses her ballpoint to doodle on a message pad. Her hand is slow and precise like an artist. "I don't know if he thinks that."

"Tell me something, Nancy. Why did you become a nurse?"

A KID'S GAME

Like so many small caves, a row of wooden booths lines the wall farthest from the bar. Reflected light from the pool table exposes only the feet of those seated there. Jake slides out from the corner booth. He smiles back into the darkness and raises his palm, signaling a stop, and then he turns and strolls over to Matthew standing at the bar. "She's great," he says.

Matthew sips his beer. He notices that Jake is wearing his wedding ring.

"She's perfect. Doesn't know anybody at the department." He orders a shot of bar whiskey with a beer back and a vodka grape.

"Isn't that what you said about Cindy?"

"Here she comes. Look at her."

A woman wearing a short summer dress slides out of Jake's booth. Her legs are smooth and bare.

After she stands, she takes a moment to adjust the dress with a quick shimmy movement. The pool players stop to look at her. Any of them would swear that she's not wearing panties or a bra. She smiles at the players and walks directly over to Jake.

"Isn't she something?" Jake takes a short pull on his beer. "Met her at Little League."

She stands beside Jake, resting a hand on his shoulder and a breast tight against his arm. "Is this mine?" Without waiting for either of them to answer she picks up the vodka grape and sucks a sip through the little red straw. "You must be Matthew." She reaches out and touches his shoulder. "I'm Jada. Hi."

"Hi, Jada. Jake was just telling me all about you."

"I'll bet he was." She tugs on his sleeve. "What were you saying, Honey?"

Jake belts down the whiskey and takes a quick sip on his beer. "Stay with Matthew. Don't wander off. I'll be right back." He walks away from the bar toward the rest rooms. The squeak of his white sneakers on the hardwood floor reminds Matthew of Nurse Nancy War . . .

Jada squeezes into Jake's place at the bar. "He's so wonderful." She sucks more vodka grape through her straw. "You may as well know. I mean to have Jake."

SOMEBODY
GET A ROPE

Matthew sits at the counter on the last in a row of seven padded stools. Yellowed cotton stuffing hangs from the cracks in the cherry-colored vinyl. The seats are lumpy, uncomfortable, and clean. He leans against the lime green counter top, faded in front of each seat where other customers have leaned on it for the past twenty years. Clear salt and pepper shakers, plastic-covered menus, a forest green relish jar, and yellow and red plastic squeeze bottles for mustard and catsup are all corralled together in small stainless-steel fences bolted to the counter top. Mae, the owner, takes a gob of ground beef in her bare hands. She pats out a couple of thick burgers and tosses them on the grill. Smoky steam rises from the sizzling meat. She shakes out some seasonings—she won't ever say exactly which seasonings—on the raw side and turns the burger to seal the flavor. The smell from the seasoned smoke will stay in Matthew's uniform for the rest of the shift. He'll smell it tomorrow on his T-shirt.

He looks out past the counter top, through the gleaming, clear front window, past the police car parked next to the curb to the green city park across the street. Two little girls skip rope in a speed contest, each trying to go faster than the other. One has a better technique for whipping the rope, easily beating her friend. When they finish, the two girls let themselves fall, laughing and rolling on the grass. The girl who lost the competition is wearing a small blue and white print play dress, and when she rolls, she exposes a white flash of her underpants.

Mae rips open a head of lettuce with her large, stubby fingers, rinsing it as she peels it apart. "Sell your house yet?" She shakes a small pile of leaves dry and delicately separates them. She slices two homemade buns and lays the lettuce leaves on the top side of each.

Matthew looks away from the two little girls to the dark burgers sizzling on the grill. "Not yet. Why don't you buy it?"

Mae turns and fills his coffee cup in a single graceful motion. Dots of splattered grease and dark wipe smears decorate the wide front of her white apron. "Like the location, but I don't need no new house." She cuts into a large tomato and places a thick slice on the lettuce side of each bun. She does the same with thin slices of onion. Every movement counts.

The front door opens and a Mexican kid comes in and sits on the first stool. He looks about seven or eight. The kid's pullover red shirt hangs from his bony shoulders to his knees, many sizes too large.

Mae slides a spatula under one of the burgers and slips it onto the bun. She wraps the burger in waxed paper and puts it into a bag.

The kid's large dark eyes stay on her. She hands him the bag. "Thank you," he says and leaves without paying.

She serves Matthew's burger open faced on a plate. "I'm retiring. Closing down."

Matthew grabs a bag of chips from a basket on the counter. "What's the neighborhood going to do without this place?" Saliva collects in his mouth. He shakes the mustard and squirts a couple of lines under his burger and does the same on top with the catsup.

"Guess they'll eat fast food like everybody else."

He wipes saliva from his lips with a napkin. "You staying in town?"

"Naw, I'll move on with my life." She scrapes the grill with the spatula. "Travel around, see some places. I ain't gonna make no million dollars working. I might as well enjoy my time."

"I'll miss you." Matthew puts his hamburger together and takes a huge bite. The juicy meat and the homemade bun mix with the lettuce, onion, tomato, mustard, and catsup. "It always tastes better than I think it's going to." Juice drips into the palm of his hand, and he sets the burger down. "I've copied your moves at home." He glances back outside. "But my burgers are never this good."

Mae finishes scraping the grill and turns to Matthew. "I guess you got to have a feel for it. Like anything else."

The little girls are sprawled on the grass. The girl who won the game is looking up at a man who is standing over them. She doesn't seem afraid or worried, just looking up staring at the guy. The other little girl has pulled her dress down and is looking away from the guy. He's a small man, narrow shouldered, wearing a dark short-sleeved shirt. He might be one of their fathers, an uncle—too old for a brother. His face is pale, nearly yellow. There's nothing wrong with him. He's just standing there; he raises his arm slightly and opens his palm as if explaining something to the girls. A jump rope dangles from his hand.

Matthew slides off the cherry-red stool, moves out the front door and across the street.

The man turns his gleaming, gelatinlike face toward Matthew and makes a sickly smile. "I'm glad you're here, Officer. I was just explaining to the little girls about keeping their possessions safe."

Matthew asks the girls if they know the man. They're both red faced and look down as if they've done something wrong. The girl who lost the contest says they don't know him, have never seen him. "He's creepy," the winner says.

Paleface holds the rope up. "Didn't I bring your rope back after you lost it?"

Matthew moves a step closer as if to look at the rope. If he moves any closer, the guy might panic and run.

"We didn't lose it." The winner points. "It's mine and it was right over there." She's very sure of herself.

Matthew watches the guy's eyes wander, as if he's looking for a way out. The fear smell leaks from him like sweat. *He's ready to run.* He'll look for an edge, maybe act insulted, and when he thinks Matthew is not paying attention, he'll jump and go like a deer. If he's fast, and if Matthew waits for him to run, he may get away.

Matthew's guts tighten down on the single bite of hamburger. The guy looks past him as if daring him to look away. *If he's going to run, he'll do it now.* Matthew turns casually. A woman with two little girls dancing in front of her walks toward them. The little girls squeal and tumble on the grass in front of the two jump-rope girls. The four of them laugh and jabber. They know one another. They're friends. The guy puts his arm around the woman's waist. "Officer, this is my wife," he says. The woman nods to Matthew and smiles. "Pleased to meet you, Officer." She kisses her husband's cheek.

The winner says, "I didn't know this was your daddy."

As he walks away, his guts burn. He slides in behind the wheel of his police car and catches a look at himself in the rearview mirror. His complexion is yellow and weak.

THE CLEANSING FIRE

Streetlights wash the color from the intersection, leaving only shades of flat gray. From the shadows Matthew watches a young guy in a dark-colored Chevy, probably green, stop at the traffic light. The guy looks around at the driver of a white convertible with the top up that pulls in beside him. The street is quiet, no other traffic, nobody walking. On the opposite corner a flexible metal grate covers the front of a camera store with a large gray A-1 alarm box mounted high on the wall facing the street. The building stands close to the sidewalk and looks like part of a jail. The bank next to the camera shop is clean—no bars, no alarm box. A few steps from the sidewalk, groomed beds of pansies bloom among trimmed bushes. Evergreen shrubs cling to a small landscaped incline that ends at a row of evenly spaced white birch trees.

The guy in the Chevy sits close to the wheel, looks up and down the street, and taps his hand on the dash as if he's keeping time to some music. He wants to go, but he's not anxious about it; he's confident but not calm; excited but in control.

The traffic light changes to green. The white convertible makes a quick left turn while the Chevy glides straight ahead into the intersection. A block later Matthew hits the reds and floods the guy's rearview mirrors with the spotlight.

He walks up to the Chevy. "Good evening, sir."

The driver looks over his shoulder at Matthew. His eyes are nearly squinted shut. "Why did you stop me?" He squirms in his seat to avoid the spotlight.

"Driver's license and registration, please."

The guy moans as if his stomach hurts and digs through a mound of loose paper from the glove box. He comes up with a crumpled registration for the Chevy and hands it over to Matthew with his driver's license. "You want my insurance card, too?"

"Everybody's got to have it."

He hands it over. "You're surprised that I got insurance, aren't you? It's paid up to date, too."

Matthew calls in a warrant check on the guy. "Where you headed?"

The guy stares at Matthew and pauses as if he might not answer. "Wedding rehearsal."

"Congratulations." Matthew notices the guy's manicure and clean fingernails. His shirt and pants are pressed with razor creases.

"It ain't mine. I'm one of the ushers."

Matthew opens the driver's door. "Would you step out for a minute? It won't take long."

"What for?" His eyes open and dance like a revolution fire. He steps into the street.

"You don't mind if I look in your car?"

"I mind." He's confident. "It's my rights."

"You won't sign the form?"

"No way. I don't have to sign nothing."

Matthew locks the guy in the backseat of the police car. "For my protection. You understand."

"No, I don't. This ain't legal."

Up under the Chevy's dash, buried behind the speedometer cable, hidden from view, a half ounce of Mexican brown heroin rolled in a zip sandwich bag is waiting for him. Matthew knows the feel of it and slides the bag into his pocket. Moments later he frees the smiling, confident driver.

"That's a bum search, man. I know my rights."

"Vaya con Dios."

"I could sue you." The guy swaggers back to his car. "Maybe I will."

"It's your right."

"Damn straight." He slides in behind the wheel. The spotlight goes out, and the Chevy glides away from the curb.

Matthew hides the heroin under the backseat of the police car. Later he scatters it in an open fire at the cave. The image of the guy in the green Chevy arriving at his party without the heroin lingers with him as dark smoke rises from the little blaze, mixes with the damp night air, and disappears.

THE TAXPAYER

At the head of the briefing room, near the podium, six sergeants hover around Lieutenant Lopath. He's telling a story. The volume and bass of his voice builds; all the sergeants chuckle. A couple of them fawn and laugh longer than the others. They hang on his words while proudly displaying their red-faced grins. Two older sergeants—both near retirement—hold a few steps back from the group. They look embarrassed, but they smile politely and stay near enough not to be seen as rebellious. Although the regulations don't demand it, all wear neckties. *Look sharp, be sharp.* Lopath is a believer. Matthew hears him say "fornicate" as the story ends. The sergeants laugh again and a few of them snort. One of them bangs the podium with the palm of his hand, "That's a good one, Lieutenant."

Lopath points to his watch and puts a finger to his lips to shush them like a fourth-grade teacher. The youngest sergeant in the group steps up to the podium and calls each officer's name from a roll list. When he finishes, he steps back and smiles at Lopath. He's a true fawner. Another young one steps forward to read the latest memos from the Office of the Chief of Police, mainly restrictions on vacation requests and meal gratuities and a reminder that no more than two officers are allowed to gather at any location unless under the direct supervision of a sergeant or the watch commander.

Matthew doodles on his notepad, mindless of the drawing until Edward nudges him. At the tip of his pen he finds a drawing of a police badge pinned to a donkey's ass. "God help us," he whispers.

Lieutenant Lopath steps to the podium; his short blond hair looks sprayed into place; the large arteries and vessels in his neck bulge as if his shirt collar is choking off the circulation. In his firm, commanding voice he announces, "Men." Then he pauses to make certain that everyone is paying attention and, in doing so, seems to discover his gender omission. "And women." He's made the same mistake many times. He's known for it. A few of the men claim it to be his only redeeming quality. "A recent study concludes that beat officers spend 95 percent of their free patrol time in the high-crime areas of their beats." He pauses again and smiles. His teeth are even, perfectly white, and rumored to be caps. "I want you to take the initiative here and spend some of that free patrol time in the regular neighborhoods. Let the tax-payers see you out there for a change." Again, he uses his smile as punctuation. He looks like a poster boy for police-officer recruitment.

The briefing ends with Lopath leaving the room while a sergeant asks if there is "anything from the floor?"

Edward leans back and rubs his belly. "I always begin to feel sick to my stomach about now."

IN THE EYES
OF GOD

A half hour before dusk Matthew gets his first call of the shift: Unwanted Guest.

The Mexican sits at the kitchen table near the open front door. He leans into his food, elbows on the table. With each breath his heavy, muscular chest heaves under his black silk shirt. He dabs at a plate of chile verde with the blunt end of a rolled flour tortilla. His blonde wife, holding a baby, sits at the opposite end of the table with three children gathered around her, their backs to the wall. None of them eat. None of them talk.

"What do you want?" The Mexican bites the end of his tortilla.

Matthew stands outside at the screen door. Behind him the three-story terra-cotta-colored stucco apartment buildings make a circle around a cement slab with a small dirt-filled swimming pool in the center. A sign listing the pool rules hangs from a rusty metal pole: No Running, No Shouting, No Diving, No Pushing, No Pets and at the bottom of the sign: No Lifeguard on Duty. "Good evening."

Dozens of women, young men, and children look down at him from the common walkways that face the pool. Their voices enlarge, echoing off the buildings.

The Mexican finishes chewing and drops his tortilla onto the chile verde. "There's no trouble here."

"Mind if I come in? It's loud out here."

"Suit yourself. It's not my casa, man." The Mexican pushes his chair back and stands. Matthew opens the screen door and steps inside. The room is too small for both of them.

The woman's eyes show terror. Her children stay silent. Only the baby looks at Matthew.

"I was just leaving."

"Mind if I walk with you?"

They step out into the plaza, and the crowd all the way up to the third floor goes church-silent like the moment of death. They walk side by side along the edge of the cement slab. Matthew keeps a slow step to match the Mexican's. "You see that nigger over there in the corner?" The Mexican's voice echoes loud enough for everyone to hear.

"Let's make this as peaceful as possible."

"These assholes don't like me."

"Normally they don't like me much either."

"You and me, Indio, we could take all these bastards." The Mexican laughs and raises his voice.

"Hey, Henry, you nigger bastard! You think I don't know what you're doing?"

"Could we not yell, please?" Matthew slides his clublike flashlight into his left hand. He knows his power does not match the Mexican's.

"You're a nigger, Henry. And a coward!"

Henry stares from the shadows. His hands jammed in his Levis, his huge arms flex, but he stays very still. The Mexican seems to feel his own power and slows his step.

Matthew leans toward him. "Let's leave this place."

"All right, Indio." The Mexican laughs and bares his teeth at Henry. "Today is not the day for revenge, but it's coming, Henry."

Outside the plaza, they walk toward the Mexican's car. "Hey, Indio, you see the bastard freeze up?" He turns his large dark eyes on Matthew. "He's screwing her."

Matthew slides the flashlight back into his leg pocket. "Who knows what a woman will do. The marriage ends. Maybe she's just trying to get revenge on you?"

"The marriage don't end in the eyes of God. It was Henry that called you tonight."

"Maybe you could have the ex and the kids over to your place instead of coming here."

"Too many women at my house. Besides, my PO says I'm to stay away from her. There is no easy answer."

"Your PO won't like this."

"He fears me like those who live in that cage. Hey, Indio, you know this is a dangerous place. You should not be here alone."

"I think we got too many sergeants tonight."

"Not enough Indians? A cop could die easy in there."

"Yes, I know."

"Maybe you could tell your white half not to say anything to my PO."

"And maybe you could forget about Henry this time."

"Maybe I could." His massive chest sags.

The sun is gone and the shadows around the front of the apartment building seem to block the entrance. The Mexican leaves with his headlights out.

BRINGING HOME
THE BACON

At the cave Matthew sits alone in the dark, sipping coffee from a paper cup. In two hours he'll drive back to the police garage and check out for the evening. He'll change as quickly as possible in the locker room, trying not to listen to the younger cops talk about their calls: who they met, who they arrested, what they did, how fast they drove, and who they hit. He'll slide out quietly, avoiding invitations to tip a few, and he'll drive Ridge Road to his quiet, dark house marked with the For Sale sign.

He sets his paper cup on the dash and answers what he hopes will be his last call of the evening: Suspicious Noise.

The old man sits on his three-step cement porch and lets his legs dangle over the side. The soles of his shoes brush the top of a rough patch of dirty grass that stretches between his porch and his neighbor's. He watches Matthew walk toward him across the patchy lawn that separates the group of single-story duplexes from the street. The complex is called Hidden Cove. Matthew steps around a car tire left in the common area. The project's design should have given residents a feeling of privacy with a pleasant view—duplexes with only one common wall and at least one window in each of the other walls—but the buildings are close together and the walls are not well insulated. The old man has seen Matthew many times before but has never spoken to him.

Matthew stops near the side of the porch, using the old man's half of the duplex to shield his back.

The old man stirs around to look at him. "You know my neighbor?" He motions with his chin to the other side of his duplex.

"No."

"Well, you should."

"Why's that?"

"He got her inside there with him right now." He points to the black sky with his right index finger. "Can't see her, but he got her in there all right."

"Who does he have in there?"

"He got his wife." The guy stares at the ground in front of his feet for a moment. "She dead."

"How do you know she's in there if you can't see her?"

He leans closer to Matthew and lowers his voice. "These walls don't lie." He nods his head. "Believe it. She cries at night. Believe it."

Matthew crosses the battered turf, climbs the steps, and before he can tap on the door he's assaulted by the thick smell of bacon grease. A guy about fifty in a green checked shirt and wrinkled khaki shorts answers Matthew's knock.

"What can I do for you, Officer?"

"I'm not sure."

"Well, come on in while you figure it out." He opens the screen door, and Matthew steps inside. The bare living room walls, once plain beige, are streaked like gray clouds. Black fingerprints smear the area surrounding the light switch. An easy chair without legs faces the only window. The bacon smell settles on him, soaking into his uniform.

"I'm cooking." The guy beckons Matthew to follow him into the small kitchen. A pile of bacon in an aluminum fry pan simmers in its own grease on the stove. "She likes bacon late at night." He stabs at the pile with a fork and separates it into strips. The grease explodes into a mass of bubbles. In mock battle the guy steps back, holding the fork defensively, like a sword, flashing it back and forth. He ends the fight with a final, long killing thrust and turns the stove burner down.

"That's a lot of bacon."

"It's for the week. Sometimes I wish she liked regular food, but for her it's bacon or nothing."

"Who is it that cries in your house at night?"

The guy stares at Matthew. His eyes sag. "Who needs to know?"

Matthew waits, hoping he's wrong, hoping the guy's wife isn't lying in the bedroom, tortured or dead. Once he found a woman tied in a closet; her eyes and the tips of her fingers were missing.

"We only had a few years together before she went." The guy turns the burner off and lifts fork-fuls of brown, stiff bacon onto a paper towel. He takes care not to break the fragile strips. The towel turns muddy with the grease. "You'd probably find it's Trouble that cries in the night." He finishes stacking the bacon and dumps the pan with the fork into the sink. The clatter echoes around the bare kitchen.

"What trouble?" Matthew waits again.

"Trouble, Miss Trouble, my wife's cat. She loves bacon and cries a little every evening."

"So your wife is not here?"

"In the apartment? Not that I could point at." He places a few strips of bacon on a pink side plate. "She's been gone two years."

"I'm sorry."

"We miss her."

"And Miss Trouble is the cat that cries?"

"Started doing it the first night after my wife went."

"Any idea why she cries?"

"Couldn't say for sure, but my wife and Trou-ble were very close." He picks up the pink plate. "It's feeding time. I'm sorry, she won't come if anyone's here."

"You getting along all right?"

"I got Trouble to look after." He sets the pink plate on the kitchen floor in a corner next to a blue plastic water bowl. "I don't know what I'll do when she goes."

"Things work out." Matthew walks to the front door and opens the screen.

"I guess." The guy calls for Trouble. He smiles at Matthew. "Like I said, she won't come if anybody is here."

Matthew stops by the neighbor who waits on his front porch, still swinging his feet over the short brown grass.

"Did you find her?"

"It's all right in there." Matthew hands the old man a business card. "I want you to promise to call me when the crying stops."

The old man looks at the Police Department card with a phone number and Matthew's name. "I will," he says. "I promise."

INDIAN GIVER

Nurse Nancy War . . . sits in the shadow in the last booth in Murray's Tap Room. Her name plate is covered by a red sweater that makes her look bulky. She wears the sleeves extended over her hands like a teenager. Her right hand slithers out to hold the glass while she takes a sip of her drink, a manhattan. "This is good." She takes a large gulp. Her gray eyes brighten. "Really good."

Noise from the pool players' voices and the jukebox music are softened like a distant small-town summer sound.

Matthew takes a couple of quick sips of his beer. "Murray makes good drinks."

"How would you know?" Her hand retreats up the sleeve. "You're drinking beer." Her voice is calm and familiar.

"It's a rumor."

"I shouldn't be doing this." She smiles and chews some ice from her drink.

"Why not?"

"You know why not." Her voice is playful. "I'm practically married." White fingertips appear from inside the end of her sleeve. She grips her glass and finishes off the manhattan. "I'm going to Texas next week."

"Vacation?"

"Lord, no. Who would go to Texas for a vacation?"

Matthew takes another sip of his beer.

"I'm going down to see my granny." She swirls the ice in her glass. "She's getting up there, ninety something."

"You're going down to take care of her?"

"My great aunt does that. It's time I let Granny know what I want so she'll know what to leave me."

"You'd really do that?" He looks away and watches David come in and stand at the bar.

"It's worth the trip. She's got some valuable stuff. I got to get my claim in early before the others. Like I said, she's getting up there."

"Jesus."

"I have an advantage over most of them." She sucks up the last of the ice from her glass. "You want to know what it is?"

Matthew tips his beer bottle at her.

"They say she looked like me when she was young. Myself, I don't see the resemblance, but I'm keeping my mouth shut about that."

He finishes his beer.

Nancy looks around the room as if she might consume all of it. Her eyes glisten. "I've always been curious about this place. It has a reputation. Everybody knows it's a cop bar. You come here all the time, right?"

"Right."

"Why did you bring me to a cop bar with a reputation?" She rakes her tongue across her front teeth.

"It's what you're dressed for."

"What does that mean?"

"It means nothing. This is a comfortable place, and Murray keeps it open after hours."

"Is that legal?"

"No."

"So you're a cop, but you break the law."

"Yes."

"Isn't that like a hypocrite?"

"I'll get you another drink."

"Are you married?"

Matthew slides out of the booth with Nancy's empty glass.

"Tell him to make a sweet one this time. Don't forget the ice. You have to tell him about the ice." She smiles. "It's not the normal way."

He walks over to the bar next to David. Murray sees him coming, and Matthew waves the glass. "A sweet one."

"With ice?"

"With ice."

"Jesus, what next?" Murray shuffles away, down the bar.

Matthew turns to David. "Do you know Nurse Nancy?"

"Probably." David looks tired. "I know lots of nurses. Just left one off at her hospital."

"She's waiting for you over in the last booth."

David's eyes brighten like Nancy's just after she finished her manhattan.

Murray glides back over to them. He places a fresh manhattan sweet over ice on the bar in front of Matthew.

Matthew passes him three ones.

Murray wraps his beefy fingers around the bills. "This is disgusting." He whips a clean white towel over his shoulder and moves off down the bar.

"It's on me." Matthew slides the manhattan to David.

"For sure?"

"She's yours."

UNDER FIRE

The weather shifts. Thick tule fog folds in and forces the sickening earthy smell from the fruit-packing plants closer to the ground. David's dispatcher takes a coffee break, and her relief assigns him a "Shots Fired" call at the Hell's Angels' clubhouse. Six blocks from the call Matthew meets him behind an abandoned Safeway. Sheets of thick plywood cover the store's front windows as if a storm is coming. Their tires crunch over the glass from smashed parking-lot lights. Jake and Edward follow them. Hidden in the fog, they watch the headlights from Sergeant Whit's car meet Lieutenant Lopath's. The two sets of lights pause for a few moments and then continue a slow, random search for the officers. Finally, David flashes a blinker light.

Lopath parks and gets out of his car, wearing his hat.

A knot, like a hunger pang, forms in Matthew's guts.

The lieutenant adjusts his clip-on tie and waves for Whit to join him. As the sergeant struggles out from behind the wheel, large brown muffin crumbs and bits of glazed donut icing fall from the front of his shirt.

"SWAT will lead the way if we need to go in." Lopath stands before the officers, his powerful legs authoritatively spread, his square jaw firm. "We're strictly backup." He clears his throat. "Give me details."

David takes a breath. "Small arms fire about fifteen minutes ago." His voice is flat, without inflection. "The victim reported that the rounds . . ."

"Victim?" Lopath closes his eyes and smiles. "The party left a name?"

"Hell no, but we have their number."

His smile fades. "There's no need to curse, David."

"Sorry."

Lopath opens his eyes. "Someone is injured?"

"Not that we know about."

"I see no victim. I hear no gunfire."

"There's no SWAT either, Lieutenant." Whit points to his earpiece. "They're all busy."

Lopath shakes his head. He grabs the bill of his hat and looks as if he might remove it but only lifts it slightly as if to let in a breath of foggy air to cool his head. "No victim. No SWAT. Does any-body hear gunfire? I don't hear any gunfire. No gunfire plus no victim equals no crime."

Matthew pretends to yawn. "I wonder if there's some poor peckerhead full of holes lying in the street over there."

Whit turns to Lopath. He places his hand over his mouth as if hiding his words. "We really should take a look, Lieutenant." The officers hear every word. Nothing is hidden in the foggy closeness.

Lopath strides toward his car as if he's about to lead a charge. "Use your best judgement, Whit. I'll be in my office if you need me." As he drives by the group of officers, he pokes his head out at them. "Whatever you do, don't shoot anybody." He drives off, his tires crunching over the glass, his hat still firmly on his head.

A couple of minutes later Matthew and David park in the shadow of a giant elm, half a block from the clubhouse. They stand together in the blackness of the old tree. The stinking canning-factory fog infects the neighborhood. Nothing moves. Matthew's ears ring.

A voice whispers like a breeze. "Come in. Come in. Don't let them see you." A man's shadow points to the darkest corner of the doorway. "Walk here."

Matthew and David slide through the dark-ness like thieves and glide silently into the black living room. The door closes behind them with a tiny click.

"I'm so glad you came. I'm Lester Williams. I'm the one who called." His voice is thin, with an unused quality, as if he seldom speaks above a whisper. He holds out his hand. Matthew gropes at it, clumsily shaking Lester's wrist. "That's my wife, Leslie, in the big chair."

Light from the street exposes Leslie's silhouette. "Good evening." She sounds tired, used up. "You see how we live?" She raises a glass to her mouth and drinks. "You can see." She speaks before she's done swallowing and gags on her drink.

Lester moves over to her and slaps her on the back a couple of times, and she quits coughing. "And the boys over on the couch." No light reaches them.

"You keep it dark like this?" David stays in the shadows.

"Only when there's shooting."

"It happens all the time." Leslie draws out the "allll" to make her point and takes another long drink.

"Have you considered blackout curtains?"

"You can't see out. They could come right up on us." Lester grabs Matthew by the forearm. "I want to show you something." He pulls him into a black hallway, with David trailing behind.

"I can't see a thing." David turns his flashlight on and points it to the floor.

"Please turn that out. The streetlight is enough. This is what I want to show you. This is my boys' room." Lester opens the door and steps inside to the shadows. Slits of light leaking in from the streetlight give the room a dusty gray color. Mattresses and box springs lean against the walls.

Three sleeping bags and pillows with extra bedding lie in a sad, neat row on the carpet.

"They sleep on the floor?"

"Every single night." His voice breaks as if he might cry. "I'd torch this place, burn it to the ground, but I'd get caught sure as hell."

"You've tried to sell?"

"Sure. You want to buy a house? Cheap."

"I got one."

"I'm all done in. My kids are scared. You've met Leslie. The last time I called the police, the cop sat out front of my house with his flashers going. When he finally came to the door, he said he couldn't do anything. After he left they slashed all four of my tires. I watched them do it. They wanted me to see." Lester rubs his face. The rasp of his hand on his whiskers seems to surprise him, and he stops abruptly. "It was my lowest moment."

"If we arrest them, will you testify?"

"Leslie is leaving me. She'll take the boys. I have nothing to lose."

"Neither do we."

David turns and gropes his way back down the hallway. "Speak for yourself."

Lester walks them toward the front door. They pass Leslie and the three boys in the hallway. She raises her glass like she's making a toast. "Bedtime," she says. "Lights out." She laughs alone at her joke.

TAKE NO PRISONERS

Matthew and David meet with Edward and Jake back behind the Safeway. Whit has gone for coffee and a fresh cream-filled donut. "He said to call when we need him." Jake laughs and throws a rock at a broken light fixture hanging from a pole. The rock misses to the right by several feet. "Damn, I'm losing my arm." He sounds as if the loss is significant to him.

The tule fog, along with the fruit-packing smell, seems to thin a bit. Matthew spits some of the vile sweetness from his mouth. "If we go in and make a case, Lester might show up dead."

"Fortunes of war." David smoothes the creases in his pants. "Nobody told him to buy in this neighborhood."

Edward crushes his cigarette and blows some smoke toward David. "What do you want to do, Matthew?"

"If we don't make a case, there may not be any need to mention Lester."

They move into a small circle. "Agreed?" Matthew nods and the others follow him.

David is the last to move. "I'll go along with you, Matt, but you're writing the report."

ANGEL

Matthew and Jake walk directly toward the low orange sun. The casino security guard faces them. His eyes are hidden in his own shadow. He doesn't nod or wave to acknowledge them. They walk up to him, face to face, and stop. He looks past them to the police car parked in the No Parking Area.

"Someone called for us," Jake says.

The security guard's eyes eventually come to rest on Matthew. "Inside," he says. "In the office, all the way in the back."

The wide glass doors open automatically. Jake and Matthew walk through a sickly blast of icy air tainted with cigarette smoke. Little bell sounds and chimes from the slot machines ring without rhythm. From atop a pole mounted on one of the slots, a red light twirls for no apparent reason. Flashing green and white lights spell out *3 to 1* in giant numbers across the back wall. Red and gold lights in the shape of a hanging eagle feather advertise the casino's name. The colored lights reflecting from the officers' badges give them the appearance of glittery party decorations.

"I hate coming in here." Matthew watches an old lady sitting on a stool dump three quarters into a slot and hit the button. When the spinning wheels stop, quarters clatter into the pan in front of her. She dips into her plastic tub and dumps three more quarters into the machine. Her face doesn't change. "We're not even supposed to come to this place."

Jake looks around as if he's trying to decide which machine to play. "A call is a call. Besides, this could be fun."

A cocktail girl carrying a round tray of copper-colored soda pop drinks with red cherries floating in them stops in front of Matthew. Her face, throat, arms, the backs of her hands, and the tops of her breasts are golden brown, darker than any tan. Her shining black hair is bound into a single, tight braid hanging down the middle of her back, and her lips are deep red, much darker than the cherries. "Can I bring you gentlemen anything?"

"You bet," Jake says. "I'll have a soda water with lime." He rubs his stomach as if he's hungry. "It'll settle my lunch."

The girl looks at Matthew. "And you?"

"Nothing, thanks." Matthew notices her name— Tanya—etched in a gold-colored nameplate.

"You'll be in the office?"

Matthew nods.

Tanya keeps the drink tray flat and steady while placing her elbow on her hip for support. "What will happen to her?"

"We're just here to collect evidence and take a report."

Tanya turns and walks away—her braid waves back and forth with each step.

Jake moans. "Man, look at that shit."

"That girl is true fantasy."

They make their way to the office door and wait under a security camera to be buzzed in. The small room is windowless with muddy beige-colored walls. Fluorescent tubes hum from above. On the only desk a black phone with a few lighted numbers rings. Two security guards—a man and a woman—sit at the desk on the only two chairs. Neither answers the phone. The woman holds a baby wrapped in a dingy pink blanket. She gently rocks the baby and herself. The man lights a cigarette.

"Cousin, if you have to smoke, do it outside." She uses her dark, stubby index finger to caress the baby's pink, fat cheek.

"Pipe down, Monique." He points at his cigarette. "It'll toughen the little guy's lungs."

"She's a girl, not a guy." Monique fans the smoke away with her hand.

"I should have known." He slides his chair away from the desk and stands. "Besides, you're not even holding him right."

She watches him make his way to the door and then nods to Matthew and Jake. "One of you can have his seat."

"Kind of short on office equipment, aren't you?" Jake sits at the desk and stares at the ringing phone. "You want me to answer that for you?"

"The office is upstairs. It'll get answered up there. This is our break room. We don't need much in here, just a place to get away from the action." The phone quits ringing.

"We had a report there was a note." Jake removes a blank form from his metal folder.

"No note, but we got the mom on video leaving the restroom. Can't see her face. She was moving too fast." Monique slides a video tape across the desk to Jake and keeps rocking. "You'll take the baby now?"

"We'll wait for Child Welfare to come pick her up."

"Wish I could keep her. She's a cutie." Monique touches the baby's nose with the tip of her finger. "I'd like to name her like *Baby* something, but she'll be leaving us so soon. I suppose there's no point to it."

Tanya is buzzed into the room.

Monique looks at Matthew. "What will happen to her?"

"That's what I'd like to know." Tanya sets a tall glass of ice in front of Jake.

He stares at her breasts while she twists the top off a clear bottle of soda and bends to pour the sparkling liquid over the ice. "You forgot my lime."

"I didn't forget." She pats him gently on the shoulder. "We use extract. It's in there. You want a cherry?"

Jake softens his voice. "Maybe we could have a drink together sometime."

"Listen to you." Tanya loses her smile. She seems to shrivel as she fades toward the door. "I got to get back out there."

Matthew steps up and peels the blanket away from the baby's pinkish face. Little blue eyes stare at him, looking for something familiar. He moves away and stands with his back to the wall. The blue eyes close.

"What the hell's the matter with her?" Jake takes a sip of his soda. "Can you tell me that?"

A moment later Monique smiles. "Look here," she whispers. "The little angel is sleeping. Have you ever seen anything so perfectly innocent?"

SUICIDE MISSION

The guy's butt hangs three inches off the tile floor, and his legs stretch straight out in front of him with only his heels touching. His limp arms hang at his sides. The fingers curve at the knuckles in a natural manner, as they should. The swollen hands copy the deep purple color of the tongue. The flesh of his left ring finger nearly covers his gold wedding band. Thin streaks of white hair plaster his face. The suicide's body hangs from a short, white nylon rope wrapped around his neck and tied to the bathroom doorknob with a simple half hitch.

In his report Matthew describes the scene: The man's yellow T-shirt with dark rings of sweat under his arms, his well-pressed gray work pants, black belt, brown slippers, white work socks, brown-framed prescription glasses inside a brown case in the T-shirt pocket, the rope and the half hitch. He makes a pencil sketch of the bathroom and the hanging body, resting on its heels.

The coroner's man touches the body and pronounces it dead. The crime-scene investigator scrapes under the fingernails, swabs the mouth for saliva, and picks a few hairs and fibers with tweezers. She turns the fingers, the wrists, and the arms, and she methodically feels every inch of the scalp, spreading the hair to get a better look. No bruises, no abrasions, no cuts, no sign of a struggle.

"The guy ties his own neck to a doorknob and sits down to strangle himself?" Matthew puts his notepad back in his shirt pocket.

"Yep." The investigator makes a few notes on her pad.

"He could have saved himself by kneeling."

She drops one of her swabs into a plastic bag. "Some people just aren't kneelers."

Matthew steps out of the bathroom and walks down the carpeted hallway to the kitchen. The place has an overclean smell to it, as if no dust has ever settled for long. The suicide's wife sits at the small two-chair metal-frame table and stares at a mug of coffee. The plastic tabletop has a gray and white fake marble design. She's a bulky, firm-looking woman—Matthew guesses around sixty—wearing a large dark blue skirt and a white blouse with big sleeves. It's the sort of thing she might wear to an office. Her coffee mug is decorated with yellow butterflies.

"I came home from work. He was in there like that." She keeps her eyes on the butterfly mug.

"Have you an idea about what time that was?"

"I always come in at five." Her index finger moves over the mug, tracing the outline of one of the yellow butterflies. "Is he gone?"

"I'm afraid so."

"I mean, completely?"

"Yes."

Her hefty, rounded shoulders relax. "Well, that's for the best then." She looks away through the old-style sash window out to the tiny backyard. "I wouldn't want a vegetable. I wouldn't want him that way."

"I suppose not."

"Have a seat, please."

"Thanks." Matthew pulls the other chair out from the table and sits down. The space seems too small for more than one person. "Do you have any idea why he might do such a thing?"

"Not really, but then he was never very happy since he got his disability and left work."

"How long has he been retired?"

"Nearly ten years." She stares off as if she's never thought of the time passing until now.

"He's been dissatisfied for awhile?"

"Yes. You want a cup of coffee?"

"Not right now, thanks."

"I'm due to retire next month. Forty-three years in the state system." She takes a sip of her coffee and looks into the cup. "It's cold." She pushes back from the table and stands.

Matthew feels the need to lean back to give her room to pass.

She takes a few slow, heavy steps, carrying her cup to the microwave. After placing the cup inside, she shuts the door and presses Reheat. Her hands rest on the tile countertop while she waits for the coffee to warm. "I thought we'd do some traveling. See some things since we'd have time." The microwave bell sounds, and she stares at the door as if trying to decide what to do. "We talked about Alaska." She removes the butterfly cup and carries it back to the table with the same slow, measured steps and sits down in her chair across from Matthew. "I guess I could go alone." She looks exhausted, as if she won't move from the chair again for a long time.

VOTING RIGHTS

A dozen battered green dumpsters with their lids padlocked down tight and shabby bails of used cardboard as big as Volkswagens wait in the alley behind the mall. Loose scraps of packing paper and Styrofoam beads swirl tornado-like in the light afternoon breeze.

Matthew gets out of the police car and stomps his tingling foot awake. "He's been out for how long?"

The parole officer looks up from the case file. "About six weeks."

"Not very long." Edward lights a cigarette. He inhales deeply and holds it to give his lungs time to reverse. A moment later a stream of smoke gushes from his mouth and through his nose.

The PO backs away from the smoke. "For his kind, it's long enough."

"Why not arrest him in your office?"

"I want his guns." The PO closes the case file and hands Matthew a picture of the parolee. The guy's face is black black. Distinct features—any moles or marks, his eyebrows, even his nose, and any emotion—are swallowed in the darkness.

"This guy is practically invisible." His name and description are printed on the back: Thaddeus Breaux, BM, 66, 5'10", 190.

"You guys ready?" The PO's blue eyes flash in the glare of the fading sunlight. He tosses the case file onto the front seat of his car and glances back at them. "You guys are ready to go, right?"

Matthew and Edward follow in Matthew's car, weaving their way deep into the neighborhood to a dead-end street: Bonniedale Court. The buildings are all two-story apartments, less than ten years old, shabby stucco, faded pink, blue, and gray with holes in the walls, stained from beds of flowering bushes that have died and fallen away. Many windows are shaded with bed sheets—pink, blue, fake tiger and leopard skin, and white—for curtains. Abandoned cars, some without doors or tires, some balanced on cement or wooden blocks, are parked at odd angles against the faded yellow lines designating assigned apartment parking spaces. When he was a kid, Matthew stole apricots and cherries from the orchards that grew here. He remembers hunting gophers with his dad's .22.

Edward slides out of the police car and lights a cigarette. "A child molester with guns?"

"It happens." Matthew looks around, trying to find a tree or a hill, anything from the warm days when he stole fruit and hunted gophers. "We should cite some of these cars."

"This guy was a burglar." Cigarette smoke hangs around Edward like river mist. "He's a fucking grandpa."

Matthew looks over at the PO standing on the sidewalk beside his blue compact PO car. "He's a parolee. He belongs to the system."

"Let's do it." The PO unzips his tan jacket. He looks anxious, a little pinkish in face.

The three of them walk toward the apartment building together. The PO strides a few paces ahead.

Dry red paint—the color of blood—streaks the gray metal front door of Thaddeus's apartment: PERV. The PO bangs on the door, avoiding the red paint even though it's dry. After a second series of loud banging, the muffled, gravelly voice of an old man trying to sound tough, "I got me a gun. Go way."

The PO draws his weapon—a 9mm Glock—crouches, and points it at the door. "Parole Department. Open the door, Breaux."

Matthew moans, "Oh my God."

"Put that fucking thing away." Edward drops his cigarette and grinds it out under the heel of his shoe.

Inside a chain rattles against the door. Matthew touches the PO's shoulder. "Put it away, man, or we're gone."

The PO's light skin gleams a wet, rosy color. Sweat beads caress his hairline. "So go." Matthew shrugs and Edward turns away. The PO relaxes his stance. "Wait, just wait." He slips the Glock back in its holster. His blue eyes are worried and unsure. The door opens.

Matthew smiles. "Howdy, Mister Breaux."

The old man's black eyes and black skin glow in the dim apartment light. His features disappear in the blackness of his face. "Evening." He swings the door wide and steps to the side as if asking them in.

Edward walks past him through the doorway. "You're not going to shoot us, are you, Breaux?"

"Surely not. I didn't know it was you folks." He points to the red paint on the front door. "I thought you was one of my neighbors."

A powerful Lysol odor drifting from the apartment causes Matthew to sneeze.

The PO wipes his eyes. "Damn."

"Anybody else here?" Matthew catches a second sneeze in a wad of pink tissue.

"No, I'm all alone these days."

Edward sits at the small table that separates the kitchen from the barren living room—no couch, no chair, no end table, no lamp, no pictures on the walls, nothing except green shag carpet. A pile of mustard greens fills the kitchen sink. "Looks like you're about to cook up a mess of greens." Edward relaxes at the table. The Lysol smell doesn't seem to bother him.

"I sure am. You want some?"

The PO steps into the room. "We don't have time for that, Breaux. We have reports that you've threatened people with guns." His voice echoes around the barren room, louder than it needs to be, as if he can't control his volume. The beads of sweat clinging to his hairline jiggle when he speaks.

"I just say that stuff to keep them away from the door." Thaddeus waves his open hand. "Search the place."

"We will, of course, but a man in your position should not threaten his neighbors."

Edward shakes a cigarette from his pack and offers one to Breaux. "I gave 'em up, but you go right ahead, Officer. I still like the smell of it."

The PO looks around the empty living room. "Officer, I'm going to search in the bedroom. He's not to leave this area."

Breaux slumps into the only other chair at the kitchen table. He looks at Edward. "I didn't mean no harm."

Edward lets the smoke drift out of his nose. "Folks can get real mean toward your kind of a crime."

"Officer, I was a thief, a burglar."

"Somebody did a deed with the kid."

"That's right. Somebody."

"But not you."

"After I went to prison, I swore I'd never deny it again. I done fourteen years, three months, nine days. Don't do no good to say I didn't do it, never did. Got guys inside that killed their mom or stole a dollar. Most of 'em says they didn't do it. All of 'em lying. Or not. It don't matter. They's all still inside."

"Well, you're out now."

"Yup, I'm out, but sometimes it don't feel that much different."

"Maybe you should get a TV or radio or something."

"It is a little quiet in here. Sometimes I just sit and listen to the neighbors." He smiles and uses his palm to brush a few crumbs off the table. "I'm saving up for a radio."

The PO strides back to the kitchen. "Did you find anything in here?"

Matthew's gaze wanders to the empty living room. "Nope."

Breaux looks to his PO. "I may have to move out from this place if things around here don't get better for me."

"If you move, we got to do the notifications all over again."

"You mean my new neighbors would have to know?"

"All the postcards would have to be sent again. Your photograph would appear in the newspaper just like before, only with your new address. Everything would be done exactly the same."

"Don't I have a say in any of this?"

"It's the law, Breaux." The PO opens a black pocket-size notebook and moves his finger down a list of names. "You're a month behind on your victim restitution payments and your parole dues."

Thaddeus gets up and walks over to the kitchen sink. He rinses his greens in cold tap water and then shakes them dry by the bunches.

"Didn't you hear me, Breaux?" The PO shoves his notebook into his back pocket. "You need to make a payment this week. Nonpayment is a serious violation."

Edward is first to notice the black revolver in Thaddeus's right hand. He remembers later that it was cheap looking and he thought it might not fire. Without hesitation or emotion—before Edward can move his lips—as if still rinsing greens, Thaddeus places the barrel in his mouth and pulls the trigger. The noise takes away everything else. The PO drops and may have hit the floor before Thaddeus. His Glock falls from the holster and bounces across the floor. He scampers to it like a baby crawling for a toy. Matthew draws his gun, turns, and points it at the sink where Thaddeus had been standing. Panic shudders through him until he sees Thaddeus lying on the kitchen floor. He glides over and takes the gun from the old man's hand. He touches the neck, searching for a pulse. The black eyes are open, staring at nothing. A pool of blood forms under Thaddeus's head. He died before he hit the floor. "Shit, Breaux, you could have waited until we left."

Edward straps his gun back in his holster. "I doubt that he could." He tears the filter from a cigarette and lights the ragged end.

UNFRIENDLY MISFIRE

"It's crazy." David sets a latte on the roof of his police car. He leans against the trunk as if he might do a couple of push-ups. "It's all upside down."

Across the street a bulldozer shoves a pile of dirt and twisted metal across a piece of open ground. "Sure is." Matthew scratches his butt. A white, powdery cloud lifts from the dozer's pile.

"How often do you think something like this happens?"

"It's progress. Old things are always being torn down."

"I mean Ed and Lopath's wife."

Matthew shades his eyes with his hand and watches the dozer back up to make another cut. "I've heard of it before."

"With a black guy in the middle?" David pushes himself off the car trunk. He takes his latte from the roof and mixes it by swirling the paper cup around.

"Hard to say."

"It's complicated."

A cloud of black smoke blasts from a backhoe's exhaust pipe. "Complicated." Matthew watches the smoke dissipate into the air.

"Do you know how it happened?" David takes a sip of his latte.

"Maybe they love each other."

"Bullshit." David keeps swirling the latte. "I mean the misfire."

The dozer shoves a pile of broken asphalt to the base of the giant willow.

"Not Ed's time, I guess."

"The gun, damn it. What about the gun?"

"Must have been a loud click."

"Imagine Lopath's wife." David chuckles and keeps his latte swirling.

"Imagine."

Mounds of red brick and piles of broken asphalt mixed with twisted metal and old splintered lumber surround the lone willow.

"Do you think she screamed? She must have screamed."

"Deafening, according to Ed."

The top half of the last standing brick wall collapses. A cloud of fine gray dust tumbles into the air and drifts over the bare, open ground.

"Did Ed yell?"

"He didn't say."

"I'll bet he did."

"I would have."

David finishes his latte. "Where's he staying?"

"At home. You should go see him."

"What's the department going to do?"

"They'll try to keep it quiet. Who knows?"

"Maybe I'll go see him."

"He'd appreciate it, David."

"I can't remember anyone getting caught screwing another cop's wife."

"Lopath is no cop."

David swirls his empty cup and looks at it as if he wishes for more. "He carries a piece."

"But it didn't go bang."

"I don't understand why Ed took the chance."

"You could ask him about it, David."

"I'd never screw another cop's wife. Even a dink like Lopath."

"You screwed another cop's girlfriend."

David tosses his empty cup into a huge green construction-site dumpster. "Crazy." He points at the demolished school across the street. "Watch this." The dozer's diesel roars and the willow falls. Black roots writhe for a moment like fingers searching for something to grab onto.

"Progress."

David slides in behind the wheel of his patrol car. "Looks like we'll have to find a new cave."

"Won't be difficult. This city is full of hideouts."

A LITTLE GIFT

"'It's the crabs, man. The goddamn crabs. Goddamn it!' I yelled it right in the living room, sitting in my favorite recliner in full uniform. I even had my hat on." Jake shakes his head and laughs. "Cindy was in the kitchen. I yelled to get her attention. `Son of a bitch! This is it. I'm quitting that goddamn job!' I was on a roll. She finally comes out of the kitchen. 'What is it?' she says. As usual, her voice is suspicious, but I could tell she was more worried than usual." Jake sips his coffee. His eyes water with satisfaction. "It was beautiful."

"Cindy didn't suspect anything?" Matthew rubs his eyes.

"Nothing. I even put one of the little fuckers on my arm earlier and then picked it off right in front of her. `Look at that!' I practically screamed. Then I went into a fit about the filth and scum and the damn job." He tears open two creamer packets and pours the white powder from both into his coffee. "Do you know what she said?"

Matthew shakes his head. "I can't believe Cindy bought this."

"She bought it all right. She said, 'Damn, do you think I could have them?' Can you believe it? What a relief. I been worrying myself sick for a week."

"What did Jada say?"

"The bitch denied it, of course. Crying her eyes out. She'd say anything. I'm through with her."

"It's only the crabs, Jake."

"The crabs is plenty enough. Could have ruined my life."

"How do you know they came from Jada?"

"Had to be her. She's the only one I been with lately."

Matthew crushes his paper coffee cup and throws it into Jake's car. "Maybe not."

"What are you talking about?"

"You been with Cindy, haven't you?"

. . .THY NEIGHBOR. . .

"It's my pride! It's my pride is the thing."
Her vowel sounds are wide and smooth like she's
singing an old hymn. She looks at Matthew as if
her pride belongs to him, as if he must feel her
anxiety, as if his uniform with its badge and gun
gives him the insight, the obligation.

From the sidewalk in front of her house, she
points toward the neighbor's. The yard next door
is like hers: green, thick, severely edged, free of
dandelions and leaves—both lawns are pure grass
mottled by shade from a twenty-foot weeping
willow in the center of the neighbor's front yard.
The lawns melt together as one continuous green
blanket. A dozen healthy rosebushes, alternating
red and white, line the firebrick walkway that leads
from the neighbor's driveway to the front porch.
Shimmering droplets of water cling to the thorny

bushes. The walkway has been sprayed clean, presumably with the green garden hose now coiled snakelike on its own raked bed of white gravel beneath a spigot near the front porch. An American flag hangs limp from a small pole fastened to the front of the garage. The double-wide garage door is open, and the interior is draped in a black shadow. Matthew knows the guy is in there, watching.

"There." The woman takes a step forward and shakes her long, pointing, mahogany-colored finger with its magenta-painted nail. She pleads with him. "Right there! Don't you see it?" Her voice is desperate.

Searching and finally following the tip of the woman's nail, Matthew locates the residue from the neighbor's washdown—not more than a small handful of leaves and twigs held together by a black, muddy sludge resting in the gutter at the invisible property line.

"You mean that little pile of muck?"

"Yes, that's it." Triumph rings in her voice like a church bell. She lowers her hand and closes the few steps between them. Her thick, sweet scent fills him. Like a lover telling secrets, she whispers, "You see, Officer, I'm from Louisiana."

Matthew takes a step back. "I thought you might be from somewhere down South."

"There's no way to hide it."

"No reason you should."

She leans close to him. "I mean, I don't like white people."

"I see." He shuffles further away from her.

"They've had their hand in ever bit of pain I've known." Her black eyes seem ancient.

"I'll go talk to your neighbor about the gutter."

Matthew leaves her and walks along the sidewalk, past the joined lawns, up the neighbor's driveway to the sharp edge of blackness cut by the shadow of the garage. "Mind if I step out of the sun?"

The boom of a metal drawer closing echoes from the blackness. "I didn't know anyone could see me in here." The guy's voice hangs in the warm air like an insult.

Matthew steps into the shadow. "Didn't say I could see you." The gray garage floor shines as if wet. "Hot for this time of year. Good for growing things, though."

"Those damn roses keep me busy." The neighbor stands in front of a gray workbench that matches the floor. A red vise mounted on the end seems to glow like the coals of a fire. Tools hang from the wall behind the bench. Each has its designated place stenciled in black paint.

"May I ask your name?"

"I suppose you could find that out pretty easy, couldn't you, Officer?"

"Wouldn't take much."

"My name is John Henry."

"Clean as a hospital in here, Mister Henry."

"Cleanliness. Godliness. You know."

"I've heard about the connection." Matthew's eyes adjust to the dark; the details of John's face materialize—his eyes: light, light blue, nearly albino, impossible to read; the folds of his small, round chin tucked into his neck like floured bread dough. He wears a forest-green baseball cap decorated on the crown with an insignia featuring a large antlered deer in a scope's cross hairs.

John opens his palm to the workbench. "I got everything I need right at the tips of my fingers. Took me years to get it the way I want it."

"Looks like you could fix almost anything."

"Anything," he says.

"I'm glad to hear it."

"I notice you were talking to our *pickaninny*." The word rages through his teeth.

"You've had trouble with your neighbor?"

"What do you think?"

"Seems as if you don't like them much."

"A man's got to hate something. My old neighbor sold his house to those black bastards two years ago. I've had nothing but grief since. The goddamn dago left without saying why he did it."

"Maybe he hated something."

"Like I said."

Matthew points to the workbench drawer. "What's in there?"

"The same as you got. It's still legal, isn't it?"

"Far as I know." Matthew walks over next to John. "Mind if I look at it?"

"I mind, but I suppose you'd do it anyway."

"Afraid so."

John opens the metal drawer. He reaches for the gun but stops before touching it. "You want to get it yourself, don't you, Officer?" He smiles and backs away from the drawer.

Matthew reaches in, and the gun slides into his hand as if he owns it, as if he touches it every day. It's comfortable, heavy, loaded—a full clip. "You keep it charged."

"An empty gun is no more than a rock with a handle."

Matthew drops the clip into his left hand and ejects a live round from the chamber. He calls in a records check on the serial number. "It won't take a minute."

"How much of this is legal?"

Matthew locks the slide open and sets the gun on the workbench. "Most all of it."

"Let me ask you something, Officer. Did you search that blue gum's garage?

"No, I didn't."

"Did you ask what she's got in her drawers?"

"That neither."

"What do you want from me?"

"A favor."

"What makes you think I'll do you a favor?"

"It's easier than talking with me."

"I've been in this neighborhood a long time." John Henry pulls the bill of his baseball cap down, hiding his eyes. "I've watched this place go from white to brown to black. It's awful." He turns and faces his workbench. His shoulders slump forward. "What do you want me to do?"

MAKING THE
RIGHT MOVE

Matthew pulls into the vacant lot and parks his car beside David's in the shade of an old avocado tree. David's fingers flash over the keys on his laptop. The words pour out onto the screen much faster than he could ever think of them. Matthew finds the tapping soothing, reassuring, hypnotic.

From across an empty street, a three-store strip mall faces the avocado tree and the vacant lot. The mall has the look of a place that was supposed to have been prosperous. Brick planter boxes separate the parking area from the sidewalk in front of the shops. Some of the bricks are broken, some are missing, and the planter boxes are full of long brown grasses and green, healthy thistles. Many of the original parking-lot lights—globe shaped fixtures on straight black poles designed to look like streetlights from a hundred years ago—are full of holes from rocks and bullets. A modern-looking halogen streetlight—not part of the original design—towers over the parking area from atop a tall aluminum pole.

David stops his tapping and looks up from the screen. "You taking the sergeant's exam next month?"

"I take that test every time it's offered." Matthew adjusts the collar on his new uniform shirt—forty-two bucks, plus ten more for the patches. The size tag on the collar chafes his neck.

On the border of the mall, a short hedge separates it from its neighbor—a modern, clean-looking two-story medical office complex. The hedge is broken down in places, and a hard-packed pathway divides it near the middle.

The corner mall shop nearest the hedge features designer leather. A finely lettered advertisement painted on the front window in brilliant orange commands attention: *All Leather Coats, Pants, Jackets, Tops, Vests, Skirts, and Playful Panties and Bras, 60% OFF, Everything Must Go!* A mannequin with rich red lipstick and straight black hair poses, frozen in dance. A short hot-yellow, high-gloss leather skirt rides high on her thighs, nearly to her crotch, and her matching yellow leather bra leaves most of her large breasts exposed. Her knees are bent, one arm stretches above her head, and her fingers extend as if desperately trying to touch something.

"Ever study for it?" David goes back to work on the laptop.

"I did once. Got a seventy-two, my personal best. I died fifty-fourth on the list."

"You should think about using your blood."

"I wasn't raised with it."

"So? They give you a lot of points for being an Indian."

On the far end of the mall, an ice-cream parlor—The Frozen Cherry—attracts Matthew's attention. Beneath the name a banana, slightly curved and without its skin, lies open, split up the middle, in a narrow banana dish. The banana is long and extends well beyond both ends of the dish. Three large balls of ice cream—one chocolate, one strawberry, and one vanilla—lie in the banana's slit. Dark chocolate sauce oozes over the ice cream, topped with a mound of thick whipped cream, decorated with a sprinkle of chopped nuts, and crowned with three bright red cherries. The front window glass displays a painting of a cherry tree. Large red cherries, as big as apples, hang from the leafy lower limbs of the tree. A sign across the top of the window advertises Old Time Flavor. "I wonder if the real thing tastes as good as that picture looks."

David stares at his laptop's screen. "What the hell are you talking about?"

"I don't know."

"Listen, Matt, unless you're planning on being a beat cop for the rest of your life, you better pass this next test."

"You're probably right."

"Don't be a sap. You could end up like Spot. Use your blood." He takes a few swipes at the keyboard. "You got to move or die. Stagnation is a killer. There are classes you can take at the community college."

A group of boys on bicycles screams into the parking lot. Some of them roar over the hedge pathway from the medical complex. They yell and race around the few parked cars in wide circles, playing their game by their own private rules. They swerve wildly at one another. The goal is to barely scrape another boy or his bike with a handlebar or fender as if counting coup. After a successful touch, one boy rides on his rear wheel in celebration, shouting and waving a free hand in the air; another bounces onto his front wheel nose down, with both arms spread wide like wings, while whooping his victory cry. None of them seem to notice the two police cars parked in the avocado tree's shadow across the street.

"What classes?"

A little girl wearing a pink helmet and matching pink shorts peddles her bicycle into the lot. She's about the same age as the boys, just a few years older than Melanie. The little girl keeps a straight path through the crowd of boys. Some of them slide to a halt or swerve to avoid a collision. A couple of the boys move menacingly close and shout at her. The girl doesn't react; her pace remains even, direct, and unmolested. She parks her bike in front of the ice-cream parlor, and with her back to the boys, she removes her helmet and shakes her long strawberry blonde hair. The boys turn silent and watch her closely. Their game of counting coup is lost. When the little girl finishes smoothing her hair, she turns, facing the boys. She lifts her hand high above her head and waves in the direction of the two police cars.

"Aren't you paying attention? I'm talking about classes for the sergeant's exam."

The boys follow the direction of the girl's wave as Matthew returns it. She strolls into the ice-cream parlor. The boys are quiet, subdued, and they leave the parking area, peddling slowly in an orderly fashion.

"I've heard about the classes." Matthew's new shirt feels heavy in the afternoon heat.

"A class or two might help improve your score."

"Maybe."

"If nothing else, think about the bucks, man." David closes the lid on his laptop. "The fucking bucks."

"Have you taken one of those classes?"

"I just finished my homework." David smiles. "I'm going to ace the damn thing."

"I don't know if I'm ready to make the change."

"What the hell are you talking about? The only change I see is more money and less bullshit."

"You might be right."

"Listen, I used to think this job was all about catching crooks. In those days nobody caught more pukes than me."

"I remember. I wondered if you were human."

"The brass was suspicious. One night a sergeant hauled me aside. Tells me, 'Nobody makes that many arrests without crossing the line, son.' What an asshole."

"That's exactly what Spot told me would happen to you."

"There's no future in making arrests. No promotion, no reward. When I quit doing it, I found out what I really liked about this job."

"The hunt."

"That's right."

Matthew starts his engine and turns the air conditioner on high. "See you at Red's. Your turn to buy the coffee."

"Can't—I got a date." He laughs with his mouth wide open. "The hunt never stops. We keep moving or we die."

NO NEW LEADS

Matthew presses the receiver hard against his ear and lets the phone ring on and on. He's aware of everything Barbara does when she sleeps. Unintelligible little noises—groans and sighs—dribble from her mouth like small bubbles of drool. Dreams she never remembers disturb but never wake her from deep, deathlike sleep. On the thirteenth ring he feels a moment of high panic. By the twentieth each ring stings him. Barbara's sleepy voice interrupts the thirty-second ring. "Matthew. Damn." The sound of her wrestling with the phone in the bedcovers relaxes him. A moment later she clears her throat aggressively into the receiver. This, he knows, she does on purpose. "Matthew." There's no question in her voice about who is calling her.

"How's it going?"

"Matthew, it's one o'clock in the morning."

He can tell that her teeth are clenched. "I know. I'm sorry. Is Melanie with you?"

"What the hell?" She sits up in bed. "Where else would she be?"

"Are you sure?"

"Yes, of course. She's asleep in her room, she's fine."

"Would you check on her?"

"Matthew, you're beginning to scare me."

"Go check on her."

"I will. What's the matter with you?"

"I'm sorry."

"You've already said that."

"Yes, I know. I'm sorry. Damn, I can't quit saying it." He catches himself before saying it once more. "We had a situation at work."

"The little girl." Stress leaves Barbara's voice.

"You know about it?"

"It was on the late news."

"I was there. Jesus Christ. I saw her go into the ice-cream parlor."

"You saw the little girl?" Barbara sounds surprised.

"She waved to me. I left before she came out. Christ."

"God, Matthew."

"The guy took her right there, right in front of the place. We found her bicycle. She wasn't even missed for three hours."

"You couldn't have known, could you?"

"It doesn't matter now. You said you were going to check on Melanie?"

"I said I would, and I will. Do you have any idea who did it?"

"We don't know anything. I have to get back to the search." He scratches at the back of his neck at the place rubbed raw by the size tag on his new shirt. "I'll wait, Barbara." It's the first time he's said her name aloud in months.

"I'm going now." The sheets and the comforter rustle, and she makes a little moaning sound. "Relax, Matthew. Melanie's right down the hall." Barbara's slippers patter away on the hardwood floor.

STAKED OUT

An hour after dusk Jake pulls up to a red and white striped traffic pole that blocks Grand View Drive—a private street. He shows his badge to a nervous security guard who stands statuelike inside a gray river-rock booth. The young guard fidgets with his clipboard and nearly drops his pen. His thin sand-colored hair, parted on the side and combed evenly over the top of his smallish head, glistens as if wet. He adjusts his pen over the clip-board, ready to take a few notes. The heavily starched khaki uniform gives him a false, bulky largeness. In an unnaturally deep voice that breaks before the end of his sentence, he asks to see Jake's police identification card. His pale, sticklike arms hanging out of his short sleeves make him seem weak and vulnerable.

Jake smiles and flashes his police identification card. "Let's keep this between you and me." He notices the guard's name tag: James Wright.

The kid's face turns painfully pink. "I'm supposed to write your name in the book." His blue eyes water and blink with embarrassment and apology.

Jake slides his identification card back into his wallet. "How long have you carried a badge, James?"

The skin under the kid's eyes turns dark as if suddenly bruised. "This is my first week." His voice breaks again, and he clears his throat.

"How do you like it so far?"

"I like it fine." He looks around. "There's not much to do here."

"Have you ever gone on a police ride along?"

"No, sir, but I'd sure like to."

Jake gives him a thumbs-up.

"You mean it?" Large beaverlike front teeth dominate James's smile. "I'm off on Fridays."

"Make it this Friday evening."

The red and white pole lifts, and Living Oak—a gated community—swallows Jake's black Lexus as if he's a resident. Large elm and white oak trees line the street in front of a long wall made from the same river rock as the guard shack. The wall is tall enough to hide custom-built two- and three-story homes at the end of long driveways. Jake has never had more than a glimpse at one of the homes, but he imagines them surrounded by acres of edged, evenly trimmed lawns, beds of flowers, hedges sculpted for privacy, rock formations with waterfalls and fountains, tiled swimming pools, and green tennis courts.

Jake parks at the dead end of Grand View Drive, which overlooks the city in the distance and a neighborhood of tract homes in close. He turns the air conditioner off and lets the soft, clean night breeze clear his head. The neighborhood below is an organized system of curved roadways and evenly spaced streetlights. He searches with night-view binoculars borrowed from the police department. All the houses have composition roofs and backyards boxed in with wooden fences and immature trees at the property lines. The neighbor's boat and trailer, parked on the side driveway, gives him the needed bearing, and he focuses on the front door of his own house.

After a few minutes he allows his view to wander back across the driveway to the boat. Jake considers it a cheap white sailboat and not very safe. When he told Cindy the thing was an *eyesore* and he found it *offensive* to have it so close to their house, she said that *he* was the eyesore and that *he* was offensive, not the boat. The neighbor, Jack, calls the thing a sloop. "It's the most fun we've ever had on the water. The kids love it."

Storing the thing on a trailer in the driveway violates a city ordinance. Jake could have it towed and cited with one phone call, but Cindy has told him many times to leave it alone. Jack lets the neighborhood kids play pirates on it and shows them how to use the sheets and sails and explains techniques for exploiting the wind and the importance of knowing the tidal fluctuations and currents. He's a weird-looking little man with tinted prescription bifocals and thin black hair that spreads from a wide part on the side over the top of his nearly bald head. All the neighbors seem to like him. Jake has made it clear to Cindy that he doesn't much care for Jack's being around their boys unsupervised: "Don't you think he's sort of faggy?" He remembers her exact response: "Jake," she said. "Leave Jack alone."

He moves his view back to the front of the house and then on to the closed garage door. His view meanders around the neighborhood as if he's out for a stroll. He stops a little ways up the street in front of Lloyd and Linda Zopolov's house. Their place is marked with a blue vw bug that's always parked in the driveway because their garage is full of junk and motorcycles. They have teenagers, and more than once Jake has called the police because of loud music. None of the neighbors know that he's the one who makes the calls. Every time a patrol car parks in front of the Zopolovs', Cindy watches his reaction, waiting for a sign that he's responsible, but he's never yet cracked under the pressure.

The binoculars grow heavy and his eyes become sore. He takes a break and pours a cup of coffee from his stainless steel thermos. The coffee is too hot to drink, and he lets it cool in the little cup that screws onto the top of the thermos. Grand View Drive is softly shadowed with well-planned lighting that complements the large trees and the river-rock wall. A half-moon rising adds to the effect, creating a scene like a romance movie set. The sound of the city is muffled to a soft, reassuring hum, and a gentle breeze keeps the air cool and sweet, much cooler and much sweeter than the air below in his neighborhood. Jake feels special.

He tries a sip of his coffee and scalds the tip of his tongue. His jerk reaction from the sudden pain dumps a splash of hot coffee onto his lap. "Goddamn!" The coffee quickly seeps through his new tan pants and burns his thigh and scrotum. A large brown stain forms on his crotch. A moment later years of police stakeouts pay off and, despite the distraction and the burning pain, he notices the porch light above the sliding glass door on the side of his house flash, just once.

He fumbles for the binoculars with one hand and throws the coffee along with the thermos cup out the window. The cup clatters on the pavement. The top half of the sliding glass door comes into focus, and he holds a clear view and waits. After awhile doubt creeps into him: *Maybe she hit the light switch by accident when she turned off the hall light. I've done it myself. Maybe she's already in bed.* He moves his view quickly to the front yard, to the street, but as he moves over the boat on his way back to the side door, he detects a flicker of movement, and he focuses on it as if stalking an animal. A clear human image lifts to a crouched position in the small cockpit and steps from the boat to the board fence and disappears into Jake's side yard.

Of course it's Jack. Jake sees him clearly—his skinny little body, his stringy hair floating away from his nearly bald head as he makes his jump. Jack is in Jake's yard. There is no doubt. Cindy opens the sliding glass door, and Jack flashes over the threshold. He's inside with Cindy. There is no doubt about that, either.

The Lexus starts and he lets it idle. *It's my marriage, my life, my kids, my house, my bed.* His insides feel gone. He turns the ignition key again and the starter barks back at him. The car rolls away from the curb, and the metal thermos cup crunches under one of the tires. All of the dark trees lining Grand View Drive seem to exhale.

At the guard's booth a red and white striped pole blocks the exit. James steps out of the booth, strolls over to the Lexus, leans down, and casually rests his hand on the door. His huge toothy smile invades through the open window. "How'd it go?"

Jake stares at the young guy as if they've never met. "I have to leave."

"Sure, Officer. Right away, right away." James straightens up. "Are we still cool for Friday?"

Jake watches the pole, waiting for it to lift out of his way. "Friday?"

"The ride along." James's voice breaks, and he strains to swallow. "You said you'd take me for a ride along on Friday."

"I don't know if I can plan anything for Friday." His head feels heavy.

"It doesn't have to be this Friday."

"I don't think so."

"I could go on any given Friday."

"Any Friday."

"That's right. I'm free on Fridays."

"Free?" Disbelief touches his voice. "I could be at home right now."

"I'm sorry. I thought we had an understanding." James turns away toward the guard booth. "I'll open the gate."

"We had an agreement about Friday, about a ride along, you and me."

"That's what I thought, Officer."

"My name is Jake. Call me Jake."

"Okay, thanks. I sure will. Thanks, Jake." He hiccups and quickly places his hand over his mouth.

Jake leans forward and rests his forehead on the steering wheel. "Jesus, I would have been walking through the front door right now."

"Is everything all right, Jake?"

"I need a drink." He raises his head and looks at James's tooth-filled smile.

"Yea, a drink." The words drift from James's mouth as if new to him and wonderful.

"Do you know Murray's Tap Room?"

"Sure, sure. Everybody knows that place."

"Would you like to have a drink with me at Murray's tonight?"

"Are you kidding?" James looks around like a young dog just released from his chain.

"No, I'm not."

"I really want to go, but I have to stay here till two."

"I'll park and wait for you."

"You will?"

"Yes."

James stares down at the street. He holds back a hiccup. "Thanks, but the truth is, Jake, I'm only nineteen."

"Not important."

"For sure?"

"It's going to be all right." Jake reaches for his thermos. "Lost my cup. You got a spare?"

"Sure." James scurries over to the guardhouse. The legs of his starched khaki pants rasp against each other. He grabs a white mug hanging from a hook just inside the door, and on his way back over to the Lexus, he looks inside the mug, blows into it, and then wipes it with his bare hand. "It ain't mine." He grins, his front teeth on full display.

Jake takes the mug from him and pours it full of coffee from the thermos. "Thanks." He raises it as a toast toward the young security guard and then sets it into the cup holder to cool. A clean breeze graces his face. "You'll make a good cop, James."

BANK JOB

Matthew lets the automatic door open. Cool air, as stale as gray marble, assaults him as he marches past the huge white support columns that reach to a plaster ceiling, twice as high as it needs to be. The combination of his new sneakers on the firm commercial-grade carpet seems to give his step a bounce as if helping him to walk. He struts through the lobby to the last of a dozen stand-up, self-serve counter islands. Cheap black pens hang from little silver-colored chains attached to the marble counter-tops, and black plastic divider boxes keep deposit and withdrawal slips separate from each other and from a variety of other forms that he has never used. He finishes filling out a deposit slip and finds his place at the tail of the customer line that weaves its way around a series of barriers in front of the tellers' stations.

Waves of muffled voices roll around him: *Tell him I'm. . . . Why not? . . . analysis is dead . . . right. . . . Bungled?* When he first joined the police department, and before he met Barbara, he came here more often than he needed for his banking. The tellers were sweet, and he dated one for awhile. She was two years out of high school, but she had plans. She attended hairdressers' school on the weekends and finance classes evenings at a community college. "I'm serious about making it," she said. A month after they first slept together, she had her blonde hair styled and cut. Matthew noticed that short hair made her head look too small for her body, and after the style job her eyes took on a brooding quality that he had never noticed before.

"We're serious," she said. "I mean it." She was a committed woman, and after he met Barbara, he never went back to her apartment or called her. He quit going to the bank until he heard that she'd left her teller job and went to work for a hairdresser. When he resumed his regular banking business, the other tellers stopped greeting him with cute, open smiles. They avoided using his name as they had before the breakup, when he was more than just another customer. The musical ring and the sexy lilt to their voices died out. They glared hard at him; he had fallen from their grace; one called him a coward. For awhile he thought about opening a checking account at another branch, but he refused to let them drive him away. He dreamed a young cop's dream of redemption—an interrupted stickup with all the tellers looking on, a shootout, a killing, bravery, and a violent arrest. He rehearsed it many times, but after a few months, things changed at the bank. Most of the blonde teller/hairdresser's coworkers, who knew that he had dumped her, quit or moved to other branches, and new tellers filtered into their stations. Even the manager, along with most of her assistants, left. Matthew went back to his usual banking as if nothing had happened. During the troubled times with Barbara, he dated a few tellers, but only when he sensed that they were near leaving their jobs at the bank. After Barbara left with Melanie, he stopped dating the tellers and remained prepared for the stickup without longing for it.

Matthew glances beyond the head of the line and notices that one of the tellers looks like the blonde hairdresser before she cut her hair. This new one makes the same kind of direct, no-nonsense, nothing-wasted movements. A thick application of foundation coats her pale, lifeless face, no visible pits or marks—a smooth Bondo-type finish, like a death mask. She and the hairdresser could be sisters. He counts the number of people ahead of him and hopes the timing of the line allows her to become his teller.

As he moves forward he hears more voices: *Have a nice. . . . Cash? Big bills. There's a hold on . . .* The blonde teller holds her red, fierce lips tight together. Her movements seem even more angry and aggressive than the hairdresser's. When she looks away from her computer, an odd touch of fear flashes in her light blue eyes. Her customer is a short guy wearing a green and brown plaid sports jacket. His dark hair is styled with a greased look, combed straight back, and hanging over the jacket collar. He might be Mexican or Italian or even an Indian or all three. There's no way to know.

Customers at other stations finish and leave. The line shortens. He moves closer to her, and finally he's number one. The guy in plaid holds his ground. Matthew considers letting others in line go ahead of him. The voices continue: *Don't worry. No way.* A familiar voice comes from the drive-through speaker. *Why not?* The voice is David's. Matthew watches the drive-through teller squirm on her high padded stool. She shakes her head.

The station next to the blonde's opens. The teller smiles at him, "Next." He ignores her. A lady behind him in the customer line pushes close. "There's a window open." Her voice sounds pleasant. The customer in plaid places a money bag into his jacket pocket. The lady behind Matthew presses against his side, trying to move around him. The guy in plaid seems to be finished. Matthew takes a step toward him, and the lady in line steps on the heel of his shoe. The customer in the plaid jacket turns to leave; he and Matthew are only inches apart. His aftershave is sweet, nearly overpowering. Matthew waits for him to pass before stepping to the blonde's station. He displays his most seductive, soft smile. "Hi, I'd like . . ."

The blonde teller slides a Use Next Station sign in front of him and walks away without looking up. She stops at the first desk in front of a glass wall. . . . *just left.* The woman at the desk picks up the phone. The teller turns her face back toward her station, toward Matthew. The woman behind the desk hands the phone to the teller. *I'm not sure. How would I . . .* She sits on a chair beside the desk. *Maybe.* Her legs spread slightly. *I couldn't . . .* She hands the phone away.

Matthew makes his way around other customers and rushes toward the front door, but he knows that the stickup guy is gone. The last voice he hears as the electric front doors glide open is David's echoing from the speaker: *You're not married, are you?*

MIRACLE

They sit back to back on the corner edge of the mattress. The boy is shirtless, his jeans beltless, and his feet bare. The girl leans against him. Her dark dress is twisted and pulled up above her knees, one shoulder is bare. They are both short and dark skinned, darker than Matthew. Both with black hair: his is untrimmed, rough and fuzzy at the back of his neck, and matted from sleep on one side; hers is long and woven in a loose night braid. Neither has any jewelry—no watch, no ring, no silver cross with Jesus on it, nothing. The room smells of mold and rot and is bare except for the mattress on the floor and a single lit candle standing next to it. Matthew uses his flashlight tucked under his armpit to light his notepad.

We come from the south.

"Mexico?"

Further south. The boy is barrel chested. His head seems too large for his small, stocky build. *Things are bitter for Indians in our country.*

"How long have you been here?" Matthew holds back a sneeze.

A week. Our baby was born a day before we crossed. We hurried to make the border for her. We hoped for a miracle, but she was too early. The boy stops, unwilling to say how the baby suffocated between them in the soft mattress while they slept. *We put her between us for safety.*

A small bundle wrapped in a gray hospital blanket is carried from the room in the arms of a medic.

The boy and girl turn and watch the medic leave. For a moment it seems as if they might stand and follow him, but instead they slump back and continue to lean against each other on the corner of the mattress.

Matthew puts his pen away. He tells them that they should expect someone from Immigration.

The girl raises her dark, soft eyes to Matthew. *She will come back to us. Nothing else is important.*